They stood entwined in each other's arms, kissing.

Their bodies sang with the need to be as one. Belana used to wonder what true sexual synchronization would feel like, because with her other lovers she had not achieved the sheer bliss that she had been told was possible between lovers who were in tune with each other. With Nick, she knew that sublime sensation.

It sounded cheesy, but it was like that old song: she was the magnet and he was steel. She pressed her hands against his hard, muscular chest and moaned with pleasure.

Nick broke off the kiss to caress her cheek and peer down into her beloved face.

"Baby, that night we saw each other again, I swore that I would have my say no matter what. You had to know how much I regretted my actions. I don't want to regret anything about my relationship with you, so from now on I'm going to just say what's on my mind—I love you."

Books by Janice Sims

Kimani Romance

Temptation's Song
Temptation's Kiss
Dance of Temptation

JANICE SIMS

is the author of nineteen novels and has had stories included in nine anthologies. She is the recipient of an Emma Award for her novel *Desert Heat* and two Romance in Color awards: an Award of Excellence for her novel *For Keeps* and a Best Novella award for her short story "The Keys to My Heart" in the anthology *A Very Special Love.* She has been nominated for a Career Achievement Award by *RT Book Reviews* and her novel *Temptation's Song* was nominated for Best Kimani Romance Series in 2010 by *RT Book Reviews.* She lives in Florida with her family.

Dance of
TEMPTATION

JANICE SIMS

KIMANI
ROMANCE

While I was writing this novel I realized that
Belana's grandmother had the personality of my grandmother:
imperious to a fault, but very funny. So this book is dedicated to
the memory of my grandmother, Ester J. Long,
who left this world at the age of ninety on November 14, 2010.

Thanks to my editor, Kelli Martin, once again for her help
in making this book the best it could possibly be.
And to the rest of the editorial staff at Kimani Press.
You're all wonderful to work with.

KIMANI PRESS™

Recycling programs
for this product may
not exist in your area.

ISBN-13: 978-0-373-86218-4

DANCE OF TEMPTATION

www.kimanipress.com

Printed in U.S.A.

Dear Reader,

You cannot choose which family you will be born into. And if you could, would you? Our unique experiences are what make us who we are. All the trials and triumphs in our lives mold and shape us. This is what both Belana and Nick realize in this story. They've both experienced heartache but believe they have become better people because of it. To find each other and to fall in love and want to build a life together was an added bonus for these two strong-willed people. I hope you enjoy their journey.

If you'd like to contact me you can write me at Jani569432@aol.com, or visit my website at www.janicesims.com. You can also find me on Facebook. If you're not online yet, you can write me at P.O. Box 811, Mascotte, FL 34753-0811.

Best always,

Janice Sims

Chapter 1

Belana Whitaker stood backstage at the New York State Theater at Lincoln Center waiting for her cue to take the stage for the final act of *Swan Lake*. While she waited, she kept her muscles warm by stretching and raising her body onto the tips of the fresh pair of pointe shoes she'd changed into after the first three acts. She rarely had to change shoes between acts, but the toe box in the left shoe of the other pair had begun to break down. Well-fitting shoes were essential to a good performance.

Tonight marked the last show in which she would dance the role of Odette. Around her, other members of the ballet company warmed up as well. Strains of Tchaikovsky's passionate score played by the symphony orchestra filled the air. The sound waves vibrated in her belly, making her jittery with excitement.

Her partner, Gideon Oliveras, who was dancing the role of Prince Siegfried, sidled up to her. Six-two and with a body whose muscular frame had been honed to perfection from years of ballet, he also had the face of a screen idol and was the sweetest guy in the company. "Ready to create magic?" he asked softly in his Spanish-accented voice.

Hearing the smile in his tone, Belana turned her face up to his and smiled back at him. "More than ready. I'm fired up! It would be nice if we didn't have to die this time," she joked. In the ballet, the lovers drown in the lake and their souls ascend to Heaven.

Gideon beamed. "Sorry, I can't make any promises. Besides, when you fall into my arms, it's the highlight of my night, every night."

Belana laughed shortly. "I bet you say that to all the girls."

"I do not!" Gideon replied, feigning hurt at her accusation. He was happily married to another dancer. He would never cheat on her, but he'd always had a soft spot for Belana. He saw no signs that she was aware of it, though. In times like this she was focused only on the dance. He gave an imperceptible sigh, and drank in her beauty. Underneath the stage makeup was golden-brown skin that glowed, and somewhere behind the artificial eyelashes that were so long and thick they looked better suited for a cow, were warm, golden-brown eyes that sparkled. Heavy makeup was one of the sacrifices a ballerina made in order to be seen by theatergoers in the last row.

"Of course you do," Belana said with a grin. She smoothed a stray lock of long, wavy, dark brown hair with auburn highlights behind her ear. "We girls appreciate the attention. Although we know you'd never leave Gwen. You're too perfect together."

His wife, Gwen Barrow-Oliveras, was a principal dancer with another ballet company in New York City. "Because she would kill me if I cheated on her. She's very high-strung, our Gwen," Gideon said.

Belana couldn't tell if he was joking or not, but the image of slender-to-the-point-of-near-emaciation, ultrafeminine Gwen overpowering her much larger husband made her giggle. Now, if *she* were the one with blood in her eye, she might do him some damage. She was not one of those tiny ballerinas who looked as if a stiff breeze might blow her away. She was an athlete with muscles capable of achieving onstage leaps rivaling those of her male colleagues. Twenty years of ballet plus weight training and long-distance running had made her strong. She didn't look bulky like a weight lifter. Her muscles were gracefully elongated, giving her the kind of extension ballet dancers needed in order to perform intricate moves. None of it had been won without hours of grueling practice.

Which culminated in nights like this, she reminded herself as she and Gideon received their cues and leaped on to the stage, followed by the corps de ballet.

The audience applauded enthusiastically, and Belana

couldn't help thinking of the loved ones she had in the audience—her father, John, her stepmother, Isobel, and her brother, Erik.

She knew they were sitting somewhere in the middle of the theater, close to the front, but because of the bright lights she was unable to see them. Perhaps it was a good thing since all her concentration was needed to make certain her movements were precise.

The choreographer had taken risks and included acrobatics that had her soaring in tandem with Gideon, who was well-known for his ability to seemingly defy gravity and appear to be flying.

They executed an airborne split, Belana in her white swan costume, Gideon in his hunter's costume, dancing to her left in such perfect timing that he could have been her shadow. The audience gasped with delight, marveling at the height the two achieved, and the ease with which they landed and promptly went into a lift in which Gideon raised Belana above his head. With her arms spread wide, back arched, Belana exulted in the moment. This was the reason she'd never wanted to be anything except a dancer—this feeling of utter elation, of time standing still, of being in sync with another human being to such an extent that you felt as close to paradise as you ever would on earth.

In the audience her stepmother, Isobel, momentarily held her breath. "Oh, dear God, don't let him drop her," she said softly.

Her husband, John, laughed quietly. "Don't worry, darling, she's in good hands."

Farther in the back of the theater, fifteen-year-old Nona Reed sat rapt, her eyes hardly blinking as she stared at the dancers onstage. One day, she promised, she would be the one up there wowing the audience. She would be as good as Belana Whitaker.

She'd gotten so excited that she'd reached for her grandmother's hand, something she didn't often do anymore because she thought she was too old for those kinds of demonstrations of affection. Momma Yvonne had squeezed her hand affectionately.

Nona knew Momma Yvonne was as happy to be here as she was. She loved the ballet. "Your father's going to be sorry he missed this," she whispered into Nona's ear.

Nona smiled, but mentioning her father had stuck a pin in her balloon of happiness. She doubted very much that he was even thinking of her tonight. He was somewhere in California negotiating a deal for one of his big-time sports stars. He didn't care about her.

"I swear to God, Calvin, I will personally wring your neck if you don't come to your senses and stop trying to ruin your life!" Nicolas Reed, sports agent, bellowed. Sitting in front of him, reeking of stale booze and holding a cold towel to his pounding head, was Calvin Pruitt, star wide receiver for the Seattle Seahawks.

Calvin raised his head. His bloodshot eyes didn't appear to be focusing. "Could you lower your voice?" he whined.

"No!" yelled Nick. "I won't! You need to hear

me, and hear me well. You're lucky management is not kicking you to the curb. Fighting over women in nightclubs…"

"That only happened once!"

"Driving while under the influence; showing up drunk at charity events. Come on, Calvin, that's embarrassing!" Nick paced the floor of Calvin's elegantly appointed living room. "As for your career, you're lucky it's the off-season. You still have time to get in shape before training for the new season begins. You don't have the luxury of stretching out your bad behavior for much longer. Janet's serious about divorcing you if you don't stop acting like a fool. And I've told you this more than once, you're getting that big paycheck because you're delivering the goods and when you stop delivering the goods, it all goes away." Nick paused for a deep breath. "If you don't believe me, keep treating your body like a trash disposal and see how fast you're fired. Frankly, I don't want to be around to see you fall that hard. If you can't be the man I think you are, I'll have to stop representing you. I don't want to watch you crash and burn."

This time Calvin's eyes focused and he actually looked pained to hear Nick's threat. "You wouldn't do that to me, man," he said pleadingly. Nicolas Reed had taken him on five years ago when he'd been plucked from collegiate obscurity and given the opportunity to play for the Seahawks. He had been a solid college ballplayer, but not a star. He'd seen some of his fellow teammates at Notre Dame become top draft picks while he had prayed that somebody, anybody, would take a chance on him. He'd gotten his wish but was about to blow it because he hadn't been able to handle the pressures. A salary he was certain he wasn't worth. With the salary came responsibilities he wasn't prepared for. His family, his friends were constantly coming to him with their hands out. And the women! Women who probably wouldn't give him the time of day if he weren't a millionaire were throwing themselves at him. He'd broken his marriage vows, started drinking too much and partying until he dropped. Spending money like there was no tomorrow. Spiraling ever downward. Now his wife had threatened him with divorce and the loss of custody of his three-year-old son if he didn't straighten up.

Tears gleamed in his eyes as he stared up at his friend and agent. "Do you think I need to go to rehab?"

Nick nodded solemnly. "I've already set it up. Four weeks in Arizona. Physical conditioning and sessions with a psychiatrist who'll help you face the reasons why you're trying to throw your life away. You say you want your wife back. You're not going to win her back with this behavior and if you're not careful, you're going to lose Calvin Jr., too. You've got to man up, my brother. Do the hard thing, and that's to admit you've screwed up and do everything you can to make it up to your family. Got me? Because if you can't find the strength to do that, it will prove to me that you've given up on yourself, and if you've given up on yourself, then I can't represent you anymore. I know that sounds cold, but sometimes you have to face the cold, hard truth before you can change."

Nick looked regretful but he wasn't about to back down. Too much was at stake: Calvin's future and his wife, Janet's, future. She had been the one to phone Nick and ask him to talk to Calvin, try to make him see what he was doing to their son, Calvin Jr., with his irresponsible behavior. Nick admired her for wanting to fight for her family and had gotten to Seattle as quickly as he could.

Calvin cried silent tears. His head continued to throb with pain and the crying had released mucus that was running out of his nose. He grabbed tissues off the table in front of him and blew his nose. "Do you still believe in me, Nick?"

Nick paused before speaking because he knew his answer meant a lot to Calvin. He'd known from the beginning that Calvin had self-esteem issues, which led to his being so easily duped by women who were only after his money. Calvin wasn't the first professional athlete Nick had dealt with whose ego was blown up by fame, making them believe they could have any woman they wanted and not have to suffer the consequences. Nick hadn't seen this coming, though, because when he'd met Calvin at Notre Dame when he was a senior, he'd been a young man yearning to make something of himself; he'd been honest and hard-working, a truly good guy whom Nick was proud to represent.

One of Nick's strengths was seeing the potential in someone and helping them reach it. "I still believe in you, Calvin." He placed a comforting hand on Calvin's shoulder and squeezed. "Now, get up, get showered and dressed. You're getting on a plane in three hours."

After Calvin had left the room, Nick sat down hard on a chair. Sighing heavily, he raked a big hand over his close-cropped natural black hair and let his bearded chin rest wearily on his chest for a moment. He had threatened to stop representing Calvin only to scare him into facing his issues. When he'd started out as an agent he hadn't known that in his job description would be nursemaid and life coach. However, in the past seven years he'd done his fair share of intervening in the life of an athlete whose career was headed down the tubes. Sometimes he succeeded, as he felt certain he would do with Calvin. Sometimes he failed. It was never up to him, though. Each individual had to find the strength to break through whatever obstacles were keeping him down and find the winner within.

Rising, he smiled to himself, thinking of Nona. He glanced at his watch. It would be around 8:00 p.m. in New York City right now. She would be at the ballet with his mother, Yvonne. He suddenly had the urge to call her just to hear her voice, but he knew he would be interrupting and she wouldn't appreciate it. His little girl was hooked on ballet. She lived and breathed it. She took weekly classes, and practiced every day. There were recitals he missed more often than not, but which he got blow-by-blow critiques of from his mother; and Nona's bedroom wall was covered in posters of ballet luminaries, mostly of guys in tights with prominent packages. Nick grimaced. He hoped Nona didn't choose guys for that reason. But she was fifteen. Try as he might to keep her his little girl, she was growing up.

He'd told her he had two stops to make this weekend, one in Seattle and the other in San Francisco, but he bet she'd only remembered the one in California. She half listened when he talked to her. Part of the reason she heard only what she wanted to hear was because she was behaving like a martyr recently. It was poor Nona this, poor Nona that, twenty-four-seven. She thought he was neglecting her because she didn't live with him. She lived with her grandmother in Harlem while he had an apartment in Manhattan. An apartment he hardly lived in himself because he traveled so often. The agency where he was a top agent was also located in Manhattan. He kept telling her that one day soon he would be starting his own agency and he wouldn't have to travel so much, then she could move in with him.

She'd been only five when Dawn, her mother, and his wife, had gotten killed in a car crash when she was on the way home from visiting her family in Virginia. A day didn't go by that he didn't miss her. She'd been the only woman he'd ever loved. Sometimes he thought she would be the only one he ever would.

Yes, he got lonely. Loneliness, however, was better than dating nowadays. He'd tried it, and it was a nightmare. Too many women wanted to get serious too quickly. They'd obviously been waiting a long time to meet their Prince Charming, and were racing against time to procreate. They wanted to jump in bed on the first date or if they were more subtle, on the second date. They scared the hell out of him. Then there were those with relationship phobias. In spite of women thinking that men were the ones who were afraid of commitment, these women took the prize. They never wanted to define what was going on between you. They wanted to keep it loose. Date and have sex, but with no strings attached. He called it intimacy without intimacy. And when you pressed them for something more than a ready date on Friday night with breakfast included on Saturday morning, they accused you of wanting someone to take care of you. Nick Reed certainly didn't need a mother, he had one; and he didn't need a wife, either. He did require something real when he dated a woman, though. No games for him.

He thought he had found someone he could enjoy being with for the rest of his life around eight months ago, but she didn't know how to be honest with him. Subsequently, they had stopped seeing one another over a misunderstanding.

It suddenly struck him. Nona was going to the ballet tonight. And the woman he'd just thought about was a ballet dancer. He wondered if his daughter listed her as one of her idols. If she did, Nona had never mentioned it. Which wasn't surprising since his daughter didn't share her hopes and dreams with him. She reserved that for her grandmother. His heart ached because of it.

His cell phone rang. He hoped it was Nona calling but one glance at the display revealed it was another of his clients. He answered with an enthusiastic, "Joey, how's it going?"

"Oh, man, you're not gonna believe this," said Joey Blake, a right fielder with the Boston Red Sox, "Lola's expecting!"

Nick breathed a happy sigh of relief. Good news for a change. Joey and Lola had been trying to have a baby for years. "Congratulations, *daddy*," Nick said, laughing.

After the performance was over, Belana was in the dressing room she shared with several other ballerinas, getting out of her costume when the door to the dressing room opened and yet another ballerina entered. "Belana?" she said, looking around the room to the back where she spotted Belana pulling on a pair of jeans.

"Yes, Suri?" answered Belana, as she zipped up the jeans and stepped into her athletic shoes.

Suri Nash, a dark-haired dancer with brown eyes smiled as she approached her. "You've got a fan, an adorable teen with stars in her eyes. She's waiting for you in the lobby."

Belana laughed softly. Suri could be talking about none other than Nona Reed, the teenager she had been mentoring for the past six months. They had met when Belana had volunteered her time and expertise at a community center in Harlem. The woman who ran the program liked to introduce neighborhood kids to people in interesting careers so they would know there was no limit to what they could aspire to. There had been a few kids in the audience who wanted to be dancers and afterward they had approached Belana as a group, led by Nona Reed, and asked her to come to their dance class. She'd done so and had been impressed with their dedication, especially Nona's. Before long, Belana was teaching the class, along with their regular instructor, one Wednesday night per month. After class the other students hurried away, happy to be leaving the dance studio in favor of more interesting pursuits. Nona Reed lingered, practicing in front of the mirror until the community center closed. Belana stayed behind one night, too, and they began dancing together. Nona told Belana of her dreams of one day commanding the stage, traveling around the world dancing, just like her. Belana told her about the glamorous side of a dancer's life, but made sure to give her the sobering facts, too. They'd become friends.

"Thanks, Suri," Belana said now as she grabbed her bag and, fully dressed, headed for the door.

"Are you coming to the after party?" asked Suri, hopefully.

"I think I'll pass," Belana said. She rarely went to after parties. It was opening night that excited her, hearing the audience's first reaction to the performance. Her friends Elle and Patrice and their husbands had attended opening night three months ago. The ballet had been the longest-running of Belana's career, eight performances per week for twelve weeks. She simply wanted to rest for the two months the company would be on hiatus, and come back refreshed.

"There will be guys there," Suri said, still trying to entice her. "Guys who aren't dancers. When was the last time you went out on a date?"

It was true. Belana had been experiencing a dry spell. After getting her heart stomped on eight months ago, she had decided to take a break from men. She had recently met a nice guy, though, and was attending a fundraiser with him next Friday night.

"Don't waste your pity on me," she told Suri with a sly smile. "I have a date with Eli Braithwaite."

Elias "Eli" Braithwaite was one of the most eligible bachelors in New York City. It didn't hurt that he was the highest-scoring player on the Knicks' roster. Sports reporters swore the Knicks were having a good year largely because of him.

"You lucky girl!" exclaimed Suri. "I'm so jealous."

"It's just a date," Belana said. "Nothing is going to happen. You know my motto…"

"Never kiss on a first date," Suri said, laughing. "I don't understand. How are you going to know whether or not you want to see him again if you don't kiss him?"

"If you're drawn to a person, you know it from the moment you meet. You don't have to kiss to know whether he excites you or not. He can just walk into the room," Belana avowed. "I know you've experienced chemistry with a guy."

"Yes, but I like to test whether or not the chemistry is real. What if you're attracted to him but when you kiss him he has bad breath?"

Belana laughed. "If he has bad breath, you're going to smell it long before you get close enough to kiss him."

Suri, walking with her to the door, wrinkled her nose in distaste. "True. I guess I just like kissing."

"No harm in that," Belana said. "I don't do it because if I decide I don't want to see a guy again after the first date, I haven't given him any encouragement. He can't say I led him on only to drop him."

"You should have been a lawyer instead of a dancer," Suri said with a smile. They hugged again at the door. "You're still going on vacation with your girlfriends?" she asked as she held the door open for Belana.

"Oh, most definitely," Belana said. "Elle and Patty and I are going to Greece for a girls-only getaway. What are you planning to do over the break?"

"I can't tell you," Suri said in a whisper. "It involves that guy you warned me about."

Frowning, Belana stepped back into the room and shut the door. She could spare five more minutes for a friend. "Look, Suri, I know you're young and carefree and you think dating a married man is daring and you're having the time of your life. But married men rarely leave their wives, especially rich men who have so much to lose. His wife is going to take him for everything he has and ever will have if she finds out about you two. If she still wants him, she'll bring him to heel. And the first thing he'll do is drop you."

Suri shrugged nonchalantly. "I'm having fun. I'm not in it to break up his marriage. It's just nice to be pursued by such a rich, powerful man."

Belana dropped her bag on to the floor, grabbed Suri by the arm and dragged her over to a mirror. "Look at yourself!" Suri smiled at her reflection. She was a brunette beauty with wavy hair that fell to her waist, a perfect dancer's body with long, shapely legs. "There are so many men out there who would treat you just as well as Mr. Moneybags, without the inevitable heartache. Get a grip. Drop him before it stops being just fun and turns into love."

Suri sighed deeply and stopped smiling. "He says I'm the best thing that ever happened to him."

"They all say that!" Belana cried vehemently. She turned Suri around and looked her in the eyes. "Has anything I've said gotten through?"

Suri lowered her eyes shamefully.

Belana knew when she was beaten. Suri would have to learn the hard way. She threw her hands up and turned and walked away. "Just be careful," she said in parting. She was gone before Suri could say anything else.

As she quickly walked through the mostly abandoned backstage area and headed to the front of the building where the lobby was located, Belana wondered if anyone actually listened to advice from well-meaning friends when they were involved in illicit love affairs.

She supposed the excitement of an affair was simply too hard a thing to resist. To say nothing of the forbidden sex and the subterfuge needed to meet for their assignations without being caught. It was too much drama for her, which was why she avoided married men. Let a married man come on to her and she was quick to cut him off at the knees.

Chapter 2

"I'm sorry your father couldn't make it," Belana said to Nona after they'd hugged hello.

Nona, who was five-six, two inches taller than Belana, shrugged her slender shoulders regrettably. "We invited him, but he had to travel for work."

Belana had once asked Nona about her father's occupation and the girl had told her he was a lawyer. She had then quickly moved on to another subject, which made Belana think her father was a sore topic of conversation. To further make her suspicious that things were not going well between Nona and her father, one day, when they were practicing in the studio at the community center, Nona had mentioned that she didn't live with her father. She lived with her grandmother, while he had an apartment in the city. Belana wondered why that was, but didn't ask. She only knew that if she had a daughter as wonderful as Nona, she wouldn't palm her off on her mother.

Belana smiled at Nona's grandmother. "I'm glad you could make it, Mrs. Reed."

Yvonne Reed was a petite, golden-brown-skinned beauty with silver, naturally wavy hair that she wore cut short and tapered at the nape. She was sixty-eight, but looked years younger. "I wouldn't have missed it," she said, dark brown eyes sparkling with excitement. "You were wonderful!"

"Oh, thank you," Belana said with a warm smile.

"There you are!" Belana heard her brother, Erik, call behind them. She spun around and there he was hurrying toward her and the Reeds. When he reached her he hugged her tightly. "Great job, sis!"

"Thanks, Erik," Belana said after he'd let her go. She gestured to the Reeds. "I'd like you to meet Nona Reed and her grandmother, Mrs. Yvonne Reed."

Erik, six-one and athletic, was dressed in a black tailored suit, white shirt, dark gold tie and black wingtips polished to a high shine. He and Belana shared the same dark golden-brown skin tone and coppery brown eyes. He wore his black natural hair shorn very close to the scalp and was clean-shaven. Belana often told him he was ugly as sin, but that was simply a sister bringing a too-confident brother down a peg or two. He was a handsome devil, as both Nona's and her grandmother's reaction to his presence attested. They were smiling widely and gazing up at him with open admiration.

"It's a pleasure to meet you, ladies," Erik said as he smiled down at them.

"Did Mom and Dad already leave for the airport?" Belana asked Erik. Her stepmother, Isobel Jones-Whitaker, whom she called Mom, had phoned her to tell her she and her father would have to fly to Zurich for a scientific symposium right after the performance, but wouldn't dream of missing her final bow as Odette.

"I'm afraid so," Erik answered, still smiling at the Reeds. "I told them I would wait around and take you to a late dinner."

"That sounds good," said Belana. "I'm starving." She looked at the Reeds. "Would you like to join us? My treat, it would give us more time to chat."

"I'd love…" Nona began. But her grandmother grasped her arm, stopping her. Smiling, Yvonne turned to Belana. "You're very sweet, but we should be getting home."

Nona sighed with regret. She would've loved to share a meal with Belana and her gorgeous brother. How often did she get to dine with a ballet star? Better yet, how often did she get to practice her flirting skills, which needed a lot of work since she had just discovered she had flirting skills, on a real man? The guys she went to school with were no challenge at all. However, her grandmother delivered meals to elderly shut-ins on Saturday mornings, a task Nona helped with and it was more important to her not to disappoint her grandmother than socializing with one of her idols.

"Yeah, we have to get up early in the morning," she said to Belana. She gave Belana another hug. "Thank you for inviting us tonight, we really enjoyed it."

Belana hugged her back, thinking that even if her father couldn't be with her as often as she wished, he had certainly chosen a good substitute in his mother. It was obvious Yvonne Reed was a good influence on her granddaughter.

"You're welcome. I'm glad you enjoyed yourself," said Belana. "See you at the center in a couple of weeks, okay?"

"I wouldn't miss it," Nona assured Belana, and she took her grandmother's proffered hand. They bade Belana and Erik good-night.

As they walked away, Erik said softly, "What a nice kid."

"Yes, she is," agreed Belana with a wistful tone to her voice.

Erik put an arm around her shoulders and they began walking toward the exit. Most of the two-thousand-plus theatergoers had left the theater so the lobby was fairly deserted now.

"You sound like you want one of those," Erik joked.

Belana knew he was referring to her desire to have children one day. But that meant putting her career on hold and Belana, at twenty-eight, still felt she had a lot of years left in her body. Some dancers continued to perform well into their forties. Occasionally, you found one who was still dancing in their fifties, but they were the exception. The human body wore out. Joints became arthritic, muscles lost their tone, and bones became brittle with age. Dancers were constantly fighting to stay healthy.

"Someday," Belana said softly. She looked up at him, "You're the one about to turn thirty-three. You need to get on the ball!"

"I don't need that from you *and* Gran," Erik complained good-naturedly. Their father's mother, Drusilla Whitaker, was on his case quite often. She said she wanted to be around to see at least one great-grandchild born. A mischievous smile crinkled his face. "Of course, if Ana Corelli were interested, I could be persuaded to procreate."

Belana laughed. "Why don't you just ask the girl out? You've been salivating over her for the past two years."

"Because whenever I'm free, she's involved with someone, and whenever she's free I'm involved with someone."

"She's not involved with anyone right now," Belana told him. "That pretty-boy actor she was dating was caught cheating."

"What kind of fool would cheat on *her?*" Erik asked incredulously.

"A fool who believes the hype about his being the sexiest guy in America," Belana answered.

"She was dating *him?*" Again, his tone was disbelieving.

Belana frowned, thinking of the flavor-of-the-month actor who had recently trampled on Ana Corelli's heart. Ana, the sister of her friend Elle's husband, Dominic Corelli, was a highly sought-after model living in New York City. She was exquisitely beautiful, her Italian and African-American heritage producing an exotic look that made anyone seeing her for the first time do a double take. As beautiful as her visage was, though, Ana Corelli's spirit was even more beautiful. She was a sweet girl who was genuinely nice, sometimes a rarity among beautiful women. And she had talent, not just posing for the camera. She was a painter who, when she gained confidence, Belana was sure, would quit modeling and turn all her attention to her art where it belonged. That's how strongly Belana felt that Ana's true calling was not modeling but painting.

"I put a curse on him," Belana told her brother as they stepped outside of the building and began walking toward the street. Friday night in Manhattan was crowded as usual. People were not in as big a rush as they were during daylight hours, though. They strolled down city streets going to the theater, in this district, going out to dinner, or just meeting friends for drinks. "The next time he has sex with some trampy starlet his thing is going to fall off."

"Ouch!" Erik laughed. "Must you be so Lorena Bobbitt?"

"He deserves it," Belana said with emotion. "You're a man…"

"Oh, no, when a sentence starts with those words, I know I'm in for it," said Erik.

"Seriously," his sister persisted. "Why can't a man be satisfied with one woman? Why does he need to have sex with as many women as possible?"

Erik, whose nature was to joke around when presented with an uncomfortable situation, cracked, "Where are all those women they're having sex with? I'm lucky if I have a date on a Friday night. Look at me, taking my *sister* to dinner."

Belana gave him her dead-eyes look. Erik hated that look. It meant she was fed up with joking and wasn't going to put up with his mess. He swore she got it from Grandma Drusilla who was the only woman who could make him shake in his boots.

"If we're going to have a serious conversation about the state of the male/female relationship, I'll need sustenance," he said. They stood in front of a small restaurant that theatergoers frequented and which was a favorite of Belana's. Erik held the door open for Belana.

Inside, the hostess, a tall leggy redhead with green eyes cried, "Belana, I heard you *killed* tonight. Bravo, my sister!"

Belana gave Julie Banks, an actor working as a hostess until her big break came along, a warm hug. "Thanks, Julie." Julie in turn kissed her on both cheeks. The two were invariably supportive of one another, as was often the case in the huge artistic community in New York City.

"Table for two?" asked Julie, her attention now on Erik. Belana hadn't brought Erik in here before.

"Yes, please," Belana said, smiling at Erik who was blushing from the intensity of Julie's stare. "This is my brother, Erik," Belana told Julie. "Erik, Julie Banks. She's an actor."

Julie held out her hand. Erik took it and covered it with his other one. "Nice to meet you, Julie," he said.

"Any brother of Belana's is a friend of mine," quipped Julie, her pale cheeks turning a bright pink.

Erik let go of her hand and Julie led them through the packed dining room to a private booth in the back of the room. Julie took the reserved sign off the tabletop and gestured to the table. "I hope this is all right."

"Perfect," said Erik. "Thank you, Julie."

"My pleasure," said Julie, giving him a high-wattage smile. "A waiter will be with you shortly. Enjoy your evening."

She walked away, her hips swaying sexily.

When she was gone, Belana laughed softly. "Oh, my God, I thought she was going to throw you on the table and have her way with you."

"She was just being friendly," Erik said modestly. He picked up a menu and pretended to be immediately engrossed in it.

Belana reached up and lowered the menu in his hands. "Don't worry. I know you're faithful to your infatuation with Ana. Back to my earlier question, why can't men be faithful?"

"To be fair, sis," Erik said, putting the menu on the table, "women cheat, too. Who do you suppose the males are cheating with? The straight males, I mean. We *are* talking about heterosexuals?"

"Of course," said Belana with a touch of impatience.

"Don't get snippy, baby sis, or I'll have to remind you why you're really upset about Ana's boyfriend's infidelity."

Belana flashed him a belligerent challenge with her eyes. "Go on, Dr. Phil," she said through clenched teeth.

"Nicolas Reed." After Erik had said the dreaded name he instantly regretted it. His sister's eyes filled with tears and she started sniffing to hold them at bay. He snapped up a white cloth napkin from the table and handed it to her. "Sorry," he said simply, his tone pleading for forgiveness. Belana took the napkin and dabbed at her wet face.

She attempted a weak smile. "Damn, why do I still do that?"

"Because you were in love with the guy and you don't want to admit it," Erik said as if the explanation should be obvious to her.

"That can't be it," Belana denied emphatically. "I did the right thing by breaking up with him. He showed his true colors after only two months together; once a cheater, always a cheater."

"Yeah, but you said you two hadn't had the commitment conversation yet. He didn't know you wanted an exclusive relationship. You told me he looked shocked when you told him why you didn't want to see him anymore. You can't punish a guy for breaking the rules if the rules aren't even in place."

"I instinctively knew we belonged together," said Belana, knowing she sounded unreasonable. "Why didn't he?"

"Come on now, sis, you know how you've held men at arm's length for years because you were the one afraid of settling down. And no wonder. You were abandoned by your mother when you were barely two and she hasn't made any effort to be in your life ever since. Yes, you *would* wonder if you'd inherited her lack of commitment. Now, though, you know you're not like our mother. You have the capacity for long-term commitment. You just need to find the right guy. And you cry at the mention of Nicolas Reed because you think you might have missed your chance due to a case of miscommunication. Sounds to me as if he was hoping you wanted to be exclusive, but you weren't honest with him." Erik paused, waiting for Belana's response to his accusation. All he got from his sister was more silent tears.

She rose. "Excuse me."

Erik rose too, his hand on her elbow. "Are you all right? Should we go?"

Belana shook her head and picked up her bag. "I just

need to wash my face. If the waiter comes before I get back, order for me. You know what I want."

Erik sat down, feeling helpless. Why hadn't he kept his big mouth shut this time? He and Belana had always been close. Their parents divorced when Belana was two and he was seven. He remembered the fights between his parents as vividly as if they had occurred yesterday. Their mother, Mari Elizabeth Whitaker, known as Mari Tautou today, accused their father, John, of hindering her career, of trying to keep her barefoot and pregnant. Mari was a dancer. Belana had inherited that much from Mari. That's where the comparisons ended. Mari had never wanted to be a mother. The housekeeper, Mrs. Kent, got Erik up for school every morning, made his breakfast, saw him off to school. When he returned, she was there to give him an afternoon snack, make sure he did his homework, give him dinner and put him to bed at night. Belana was too young to remember the neglect by their mother, but he hadn't been. Mari couldn't even fake affection. He had felt loved by their father, but he had felt like an inconvenience to his mother. Those were not warm memories. He thanked God he had Mrs. Kent and his grandmother, Drusilla, as mother figures. Drusilla was kind enough not to deride his mother in his presence, even though he was quite sure Drusilla didn't like her. Now that he was an adult, Drusilla no longer held her tongue on the subject of Mari. She'd told him he had better not marry a woman simply because she was beautiful. His choice had better have something wonderful going for her other than her looks. "Your father was blinded by your mother's looks," Drusilla said of Mari. "If he had bothered to look deeper he wouldn't have had anything to do with her." Then she had smiled and gently rubbed his cheek. "He did get two good things out of his marriage, you and Belana."

Erik sighed deeply. The reason he had made Belana face her feelings for Nicolas Reed was because if she had dropped him because she feared commitment, and the misunderstanding that broke them up was not as monumental as Belana had described it, then she was allowing her mother to win. Allowing Mari to have an adverse affect on her life, when Mari never wanted to be a *part* of her life made no sense to Erik. By no means should Mari have that much influence. He would do everything in his power to prevent it.

The waiter arrived. He cleared his throat because Erik was still deep in his own thoughts. "Good evening, sir. Would you like to hear the specials?"

"No," said Erik. "Just bring me two cheeseburgers, fries and vanilla milk shakes."

Belana liked comfort food after a show closed. Something in her was in mourning whenever a show ran its course. Carbohydrates gave her an emotional boost. Plus, she only splurged a few times a year; every other day of the year she stuck to a healthy diet.

"Right away, sir," said the waiter, a thin, middle-aged black man with a thin, graying mustache and absolutely no hair on his head. He wore the customary uniform consisting of a white shirt, black slacks and black comfortable shoes.

When Belana returned, looking refreshed, she sat down to a meal that had just been brought to their table. She smiled at her brother. "You're an angel."

Erik smiled knowingly. "Running an extra five miles is worth it." He, too, liked to stay in shape.

They both said silent prayers before beginning to eat. Erik watched Belana attack her burger and smiled. "So what did you decide in the bathroom? To continue our conversation or ignore it altogether?"

Belana swallowed. She wiped some burger juices away from the corner of her mouth with the cloth napkin. "I'm not going to ignore it. But what can I do? It's been eight months, he's probably moved on. He was dating someone else when I ran into them, remember?"

"That doesn't mean he's dating her now," Erik said around a mouthful of burger. Belana frowned at his poor table manners. When they were kids he used to gross her out by showing her the food in his mouth while he was eating. At least he'd stopped doing that.

Seeing her expression, Erik swallowed and took a sip of his milk shake while he awaited her response. When she still didn't say anything, he said, "Chicken?"

"I would be humiliated if I phoned him to try to get back together with him and he's involved with someone else," she admitted. She took a big bite of burger and chewed slowly, very slowly, letting her brother know that she would not be replying to any antagonistic questions any time soon.

Erik knew her, though, and decided to eat in silence.

When her plate was clean, she would have no excuse not to answer his questions.

Halfway through their meal, Julie sauntered over to their table. "Is everything to your satisfaction?" she asked, smiling at Erik.

Erik was pleased to be interrupted. His sister wasn't making an effort to be a pleasant dinner companion. "Hi, Julie," he said, giving her the benefit of his sexiest smile. "Yes, thank you, everything's great."

Julie sighed and tossed her long, wavy red tresses over her shoulder. "Okay," she said, drawing out the word as if she were reluctant to have to go. "Let me know if you need anything, and I mean *anything*."

Belana noticed the stress she'd put on the word "anything" and had nearly choked on a fry. Her brother, charming devil, smiled suggestively at Julie, and said, "I surely will."

Belana kicked him underneath the table.

When Julie had gone, Erik frowned at his sister. "That hurt."

"I meant it to hurt," Belana told him. Finished eating, she pushed her plate aside and pulled her milk shake forward to concentrate on it. "If you're serious about Ana, you can't go around flirting with waitresses. You see? That's what I mean about men. I thought you loved Ana, and yet you can't resist toying with the affections of an innocent bystander."

Erik laughed shortly. "Who said I was in love with Ana? I am in fantasy-love with Ana. There's a difference. And there's no harm in a little flirting."

"Until you take it to the next step, and believe me, Julie wants to take it to the next step. If you're serious about Ana, I'll help you. But I'm not going to help you get a date with Ana if you insist on behaving like a hound. She's been hurt enough by men who didn't know how to be faithful to one woman."

"She has?" Erik asked.

"Don't you know it's the bane of the beautiful woman's existence? Men want to be with beautiful women because they look good on their arms and make them the envy of other men. But beautiful women have a very hard time finding that one special guy who'll love them for what's inside, not for how they look."

"Ana told you she'd been hurt before pretty-boy actor broke her heart?"

"A couple of times," Belana told him. "So if you're going to win Ana's heart, you need to be unimpressed by her looks and get to know who she is on the inside."

There was a contemplative expression on Erik's face. He twirled his straw around in his milk shake, thinking. Then he looked across the table and met his sister's eyes. "I'd never do anything to hurt her."

Belana smiled, satisfied. "I'm glad to hear it. She's going to be back in town in about three weeks. I'll invite you both to dinner."

"No," said Erik.

"No?" cried Belana, surprised he would object to her fixing him up with the woman of his dreams.

"No," her brother repeated. "A dinner designed for us to be in the same room at the same time, and it's just the two of us invited, will look contrived. I'll wait until one of the family dinners during the holidays when there will be lots of people around. I don't want her guard up before I can even begin to plead my case."

"It's your call," Belana said, resigned. "But it's August. There are three months before Thanksgiving. What if she meets someone else?"

"She won't," Erik said confidently. "We're meant to be together, I feel it."

"I felt that way about Nick," Belana reminded him. "But he apparently didn't."

"That you know of," countered Erik. "You're too chicken to ask him."

"Yes, I am," said Belana.

"Then you'll never know," said Erik with a sad note to his voice. "Look, Belana, I can't force you to do anything, but I have to say this. If you can't get over your cowardice and go after Nicolas Reed if you really want him, then Mari wins. Even though she has managed to stay out of your life all these years, she will have ruined it."

The arrival of their waiter saved Belana from having to reply to that. "Can I get you anything else?" he politely asked.

"No," Erik told him. "Thank you."

The waiter promptly placed the check on the table. "Thank you for your patronage. Please come again." He smiled faintly and walked away.

Erik picked up the check, put a nice tip on the table, and rose. Belana picked up her bag. She sensed her brother's mood. He was disappointed in her. She hated it when he put her on a pedestal, behaving as if she couldn't have flaws in her character like normal people. So, she was being a bit of a coward and protecting her heart when it came to Nicolas Reed. Did that make her a bad person? No!

Erik turned his back on her and began making his way to the front of the restaurant where he intended to pay the bill.

"I'll think about it," Belana blurted.

He stopped, turned and smiled at her. "Come here," he said.

She went into his outstretched arms and they hugged. "You've got to stop manipulating me with emotional blackmail," she complained.

"What are brothers for?" he asked with a smile.

Chapter 3

"**M**ykonos," Belana repeated into the cell phone's receiver.

On her end, Patrice Sutton-McKenna said, "Yes, Mykonos. I've made arrangements for us to stay at a resort there. Didn't you get my email? I sent you the resort's website so you could check out the accommodations."

"When did you send it?" asked Belana. She was fastening a diamond bracelet around her right wrist as she talked with the phone held firmly between her left ear and her shoulder. In less than ten minutes Eli Braithwaite was supposed to pick her up for their first date. "I haven't been online all day."

Patrice sighed. Belana was one of those people who

actually preferred phoning everyone instead of emailing them. "I sent it this morning. Check your mail. Elle and I will meet you at the ferry."

"Elle's going to get there before I do? She's bringing Ari with her, right? I haven't seen my niece in months."

"Yes, she's bringing the little princess with her," Patrice said. "But it'll still be just us girls, no boys allowed."

"That's cool," Belana said. "I just want to be pampered. I *will* be pampered, won't I?"

Patrice laughed shortly. "Yes, your highness, you will be in the lap of luxury. Anything your heart desires will be at your disposal."

"Just so there's a masseuse on the hotel's staff," Belana said. "My poor body could use a good massage."

"No worries," Patrice assured her. "So, what time do you think you'll be here?"

"I should be there around eleven in the morning, your time," Belana told her. "Hey, do you have any news for us?"

"What kind of news?" Patrice asked, suspicious.

"Baby news?" said Belana expectantly. A glance at the alarm clock on the nightstand in her bedroom told her she didn't have time for word games.

"I'm scheduled to shoot two films in the next six months," Patrice said with a laugh.

"That never stopped Angelina Jolie," Belana persisted.

"You're asking me, how about you?" Patrice said, turning the tables. "You're the same age as I am. When are *you* going to have a baby?"

"I'd like to catch a man first."

"What are you using for bait?"

"My usual exceptionally talented self," Belana replied jokingly.

"Any interesting prospects?" asked Patrice.

Belana told Patrice about her date with Eli Braithwaite. "We're going to a fundraiser that the Knicks throw every year to raise money to send inner-city kids to college."

"How old is he?" Patrice wanted to know.

"He's twenty-five."

"Three years younger than you."

"That doesn't make me a cougar."

"No, not at all, but let's hope he's a mature twenty-five. You know you get bored easily."

"I've improved in that department. I'm determined to find my soul mate, get married and have a child or two."

"You sound so convincing," Patrice intoned, sounding unconvinced.

Belana laughed. "As one of my oldest and dearest friends, you're supposed to show support instead of deriding me."

"As one of your oldest and dearest friends, I'm supposed to tell you the truth. Call me when you get back from your date. I'd like to know how that twenty-five-year-old boy held up to your adult sensibilities."

"He seemed mature when I met him at a fashion show. Ana introduced us."

"How much time did you spend with him?"

"About thirty minutes and then he asked me out."

Patrice harrumphed. "You've never been attracted to boys. You might think they're pretty and flirt with them but when you date, you prefer really strong, highly confident *men*. They're the only kind who can put up with you."

"Put up with me?" Belana cried, laughing. "You make me sound high-maintenance."

"You are," Patrice said, telling it like it was. "Just call me later and we'll finish this conversation then."

The doorbell rang. "Okay, talk to you later," Belana said hurriedly.

"That's Eli, huh?" said Patrice.

"Yeah, got to go," said Belana, in even more of a rush.

"I bet he brought flowers *and* candy. Oh, and a teddy bear," Patrice joked. "Little boys always overcompensate because they want to be liked."

"Bye, Miss Smarty Pants," said Belana, and hung up on Patrice.

In her bedroom, Belana quickly shoved her cell phone into her clutch and stood in front of the full-length mirror one more time. She wore an off-white sleeveless dress that had a square neckline, which revealed a hint of cleavage, and whose hem fell two inches above her knees. It was well-made, but not a designer original. She spent money sparingly on designers, preferring instead to go with quality clothing she could find at any major department store. She did have a weakness for designer shoes, however. She bought them when they went on sale. Even though her father was a millionaire many times over, and she and Erik would never lack for money, they had been brought up not to be wasteful. Money, their father taught them, was to be used for a purpose, not simply to satisfy your whims. She had favorite charities she contributed to on a regular basis, and she liked spoiling friends and family on occasion with gifts that were unexpected and truly appreciated.

She peered down at her Jimmy Choos, a pair of strappy, off-white sandals. With the extra three inches their heels provided, her head might be even with Eli's shoulders.

When she opened the door, she silently gave Patrice her due. Eli, all six feet seven inches of him, was wearing a beautiful black tuxedo and highly polished dress shoes. He was carrying a bouquet of red roses, a box of Godiva chocolate truffles and a huge, fluffy, white teddy bear with a red velvet ribbon tied around its neck.

Belana smiled broadly and asked him in. His Calvin Klein for Men preceded him into the room, but it wasn't overpowering. She had been right about their heights. She had to tiptoe to briefly hug him hello. Then he was pressing the gifts into her arms. "You look beautiful," he said in his deep baritone, his eyes raking over her.

"Thank you. You look very handsome tonight,"

Belana said as she clutched his offerings to her chest. She glanced at them a moment, then raised her eyes back to his. "You're too generous. But I love roses and chocolate's one of my guilty pleasures."

She squeezed the teddy bear. "And he's just adorable."

"I'm glad you like them," Eli said, giving her a boyish grin. He was a good-looking guy with dark-chocolate skin, chiseled facial features that reminded her of Tyson Beckford's. The two men had the same sort of dark brown eyes with an Asian aspect to them.

"Have a seat while I put these in water, then we can go," Belana suggested. She turned and fled to the kitchen. Once in the kitchen, she took a deep breath and set everything on the counter next to the sink. Reaching up into the cabinet over the sink, she retrieved a crystal vase and ran a little water into it.

"Patrice doesn't have to be right," she muttered as she put the roses into the vase one at a time. "He's sweet."

Because she lived in midtown Manhattan, it didn't take them long to reach the St. Regis on Fifth Avenue. The affair was held on the twentieth floor. The huge room was beautifully lit by crystal chandeliers and sheer, white curtains hung at the floor-to-ceiling windows.

About two hundred people sat at tables with white linen tablecloths where their names had been handwritten on tiny placards and put at their place settings. Belana and Eli were seated at a table with three other couples. Introductions were made after which Belana made polite conversation with a matronly woman with white hair who wore a vintage Chanel suit in a pale pink, pebbled fabric. Belana was fond of vintage clothing and complimented the woman on her suit.

"Oh, darling," said the woman in a thick New York accent, "this thing has seen me through every presidency since Kennedy. I bought it when Jackie was First Lady. I so admired her style. This suit has outlasted three husbands."

Belana smiled at the woman's analogy. It seemed a good suit was more reliable than some men. A cynical view, but an amusing one.

"Well, it has definitely held up over the years," Belana said.

They chatted throughout the meal which was delicious: prime rib, twice-baked potatoes, broccoli and cauliflower florets, and for dessert, New York cheesecake with fresh strawberries.

After the meal, several of the players got up and told jokes about their coach. It seemed that the fundraiser doubled as a roast. Following the roast, even though there was a band and a dance floor, everyone stood around and conversed over after-dinner drinks. The topic of conversation was invariably basketball. Belana tried her best to look interested, but she was almost relieved when her bladder started complaining and she had to excuse herself to go to the ladies' room.

She took her time freshening up. Just before leaving the powder room, she looked into the mirror to make sure her upswept hairdo had not bowed to gravity too much over the course of the evening. She rearranged tendrils of her long auburn hair, applied more lipstick, then rejoined Eli and the others.

As she approached the group of men Eli was conversing with, she noticed the back of a man she hadn't noticed before. He wore his suit well, and although he wasn't as tall as some of the players, he was otherwise physically their match. There was something awfully familiar about those broad shoulders and the confident manner in which he carried himself.

When she got closer she noticed that he had a beard, one of those very short, neatly trimmed beards that amounted to little more than a few days' growth. On some men it looked sexy, as it did on this man, or maybe it was the whole package. From this angle he was utterly masculine-looking. He had a classic profile with a strong, square-shaped jaw, high cheekbones, a rather large nose, and full lips. Plus, he had the kind of rich, dark-chocolate skin she was attracted to in a man. Belana moved around so that she could see his face, then she raised her eyes and nearly gasped out loud.

Nicolas Reed. *What is he doing here?* she screamed in her head. Eli put a possessive arm about her shoulders. She was grateful to have someone to lean on.

Her brain made the connection: Nicolas was a sports agent. This event had a lot of athletes in attendance. *Oh, Lord, don't let him be…* she was thinking when Eli cleared his throat and said, "Belana, I'd like you to meet my agent, Nicolas Reed." He proudly said this as if Nicolas were someone he greatly admired. "Nick, this is my date, Belana Whitaker. Belana's a principal dancer with the New York City Repertory Dance Theatre."

Belana tried to smile as she raised her hand to shake Nicolas's. "Mr. Reed," she said coolly.

"Miss Whitaker," Nicolas said, equally coolly. Their eyes met and Belana could see he was just as shocked to see her as she was to see him. *Good,* she thought, *at least I'm not the only one with a racing heart and sweaty palms.*

In the ensuing silence, Eli tried to break the ice with, "I think ballet dancers have to be good athletes to perform the way they do." He smiled down at Belana. "I know I couldn't do what you do."

"We definitely wouldn't want to see you in a tutu," quipped Nicolas. The other four men laughed uproariously at this, while Nick's dark brown eyes raked over Belana in a sensual caress that made her heart beat even faster. "Really, Eli, ballet is admittedly beautiful to watch but you couldn't refer to it as a sport, or the dancers as athletes. It's an art form. Wouldn't you agree, Miss Whitaker?"

Belana held her irritation in check. So that was how he wanted to play it: go along with her apparent desire to pretend they didn't know each other. It would be uncomfortable for her to have to explain their association to Eli, and he knew it. He would have his fun, though, by sending subtle digs her way.

"All I know is," Belana said very deliberately, "that

after twenty years of ballet, I've sustained numerous injuries, have often worked myself to exhaustion, my body drenched in sweat, and I have a chiropractor on call."

"Sounds like an athlete to me," said one of the gentlemen standing in their circle. Belana thought she'd heard someone say he was the team's chiropractor. His comment elicited a chuckle or two from everyone.

"Of course she's an athlete," said Eli, smiling down at Belana with something like worship in his gaze. Belana groaned inwardly. That's all she needed, having to deal with a smitten date and an angry ex simultaneously. Maybe she could find some excuse to leave, or at the very least a way to get out of Nick's presence.

She smiled up at Eli. "Dance with me?"

The band was playing a very nice version of Norah Jones's "Come Away with Me."

To her surprise, Eli blushed, and ducked his head. "I'd love to dance with you, Belana, but I'm sorry to say I've got two left feet."

Another of his friends laughed good-naturedly. "Big men rarely have any rhythm. Our feet are too big."

"Don't be ridiculous," Belana said, smiling at all of them. "I've seen the fancy footwork you use on the court!"

She grasped Eli's hand. "Come on, I'll teach you."

He was putty in her hands. He let her lead him on to the dance floor and show him how to hold her while they attempted a simple two-step. He stepped on her toes four times inside of three minutes. With each misstep he looked more embarrassed. Belana, not wanting to put him through the agony any longer, didn't protest when he said, "We'd better stop before I injure you."

She got up on the balls of her feet and kissed him on the cheek. "It was sweet of you to try."

"Anything for you, Belana," he said, smiling shyly.

Belana felt terrible as they walked back to his group of friends. She had put him through that bit of humiliation all because she hadn't wanted to face Nick.

As if she'd conjured him up by thinking of him, Nick was suddenly standing in front of them. He glanced at her, but addressed Eli. "I'll dance with Miss Whitaker if it's all right with you, Eli."

Eli looked relieved and grateful all at once. He smiled down at Belana. "If it's okay with Belana," he said.

Belana didn't see how she could refuse without appearing rude. Nick was Eli's agent and obviously his friend, too. "I'd be delighted," she said with convincing politeness.

Nick took her by the arm and led her back on to the dance floor. The band had finished the Norah Jones number and had begun the standard, "When I Fall in Love."

As soon as he pulled her into his arms she knew she was not dealing with an amateur.

His waltz was impeccable. She relaxed a bit in his arms. She hadn't known he could dance. For the first few minutes they didn't say anything, simply let their bodies move to the music. Then Nick said, "You colored your hair."

Belana lifted her head and looked him in the eyes. "You grew a beard."

Nick's expression was tender as he met her gaze. His emotions had run the gamut for the past few minutes. Upon seeing her enter the room and then be introduced as Eli's date, he had been outraged. Anger had rushed through him so rapidly and with such force that it had rocked him to the core. Why was he still angry with her after eight months? Her presence here was unexpected, but that shouldn't have elicited such a reaction from him. New York was a big city, but it wasn't unusual to run into people you were trying to avoid. It happened.

Earlier, while they stood talking to several other guests, he had been analyzing his emotions, and he'd come to the conclusion that he still felt anger toward Belana Whitaker because he'd never had the chance to have his say after she'd dumped him. She'd run out of the restaurant and climbed into a waiting taxi. He'd been unable to hail another one fast enough to follow.

Repeated phone calls had gone unanswered, messages not returned. Short of stalking her, he had been helpless to communicate with her. And he was not the stalking type. Nor the begging type. She had made the decision to stop seeing him and he had not forced the issue. However, the fact that she had not even stuck around to hear his side of the story when she'd caught him having dinner with another woman stuck in his craw. He wanted his chance to explain.

"Is this thing with Eli serious?" he asked before he really got down and dirty.

Belana's eyes met his. "It's our first date. We haven't even…"

"Kissed," Nick finished for her. "I remember you don't kiss on the first date." He narrowed his eyes at her. "At least not a real kiss. You just gave Eli a kiss on the cheek."

"Jealous?" Belana asked, smiling at him.

"A little," said Nick nonchalantly. "As I recall, I didn't even get a handshake on our first date." He gave her an inquisitive look. "So, you're dating younger men these days? Eli's barely legal."

"He told me he was twenty-five!"

"He lied," Nick stated bluntly. "What twenty-two-year-old *wouldn't* lie to date you?"

"Still," Belana said, casting a glance over her shoulder in Eli's direction. He was engrossed in conversation with his boys. "That makes me six years older than he is."

"Don't be mad at him," Nick said. He pulled her a little closer. "Now that I have your undivided attention, I've got something to say," he whispered in a steely voice.

Belana's first reaction at hearing the menace in his tone was to push out of his embrace, but he held her firmly.

"Don't make a scene," Nick said. "This won't take

long." He tried not to be moved by the panicked look in Belana's big brown eyes. "Calm down," he said softly. "Nothing's going to be hurt but your pride, although mine will get a much-needed boost."

Belana continued to stare up at him, speechless. But she exhaled and relaxed a little.

Sensing that she was willing to cooperate, Nick continued. "Good. That night you caught me having dinner with another woman was the first time I'd seen her. And witnessing the way I ran after you convinced her that it should be the last time."

Belana was inordinately happy to hear that. She had to school her features to keep from smiling. She continued to gaze up at him intently, hanging on his every word.

"For a long time after you and I stopped seeing each other," Nick said, "I thought I had been justified in dating someone else. You and I hadn't talked about dating exclusively. But later, I realized I shouldn't have been dating her when I was seeing you, even if you and I weren't exclusive."

"You did what millions of single people do," Belana said to be fair. "You were keeping your options open."

"I didn't *want* my options open," Nick said vehemently, the expression in his deep brown eyes so compelling she couldn't tear her gaze away from his. She felt weak in the knees and lightheaded with happiness. "If you had told me how you felt about us, I never would have asked her out."

Belana's heart thudded as she tried to compose what she should say next in her head. Should she simply tell him that she felt the same way, which she did? Or should she tell him the whole truth? If this was heading toward reconciliation, she owed it to him to be completely honest.

She cleared her throat. "Nick, you're not going to like this, but I need to tell you exactly why I behaved the way I did that night. Part of me was angry at you for dating someone behind my back, and I truly did feel betrayed. Another part of me was relieved it happened."

"Why?" Nick asked, frowning, and clearly confused. "Why would ending it with me make you feel relieved if you actually wanted to *be* with me?"

Belana noticed the song was coming to a close. Out of the corner of her eye she saw Eli approaching the dance floor. He obviously was anticipating the song ending, too.

Belana sighed regrettably. "I don't have time to explain."

"When I Fall in Love" ended and the band began playing an upbeat number. "Make some excuse and meet me downstairs in the bar."

"I can't do that," Belana whispered. "Eli's watching us like a hawk. Something's made him suspicious."

"Then call me when you get home tonight," he said urgently. "You still have my number, don't you?"

"Yes," said Belana softly.

"I don't care how late," Nick said as he led her off the dance floor.

Smiling warmly, Eli approached them and placed his hand beneath Belana's elbow, reclaiming her. "That looked like fun. I'm definitely going to have to take dance lessons," he said. While his tone was friendly, Belana noticed the expression in his eyes when he regarded Nick was not so friendly.

"Thanks for the dance, Miss Whitaker," Nick said.

"It was my pleasure, Mr. Reed," Belana said politely.

Nick offered Eli his hand to shake. "Thanks for inviting me tonight, Eli. But I have to be going." He smiled at them. "Enjoy your evening."

He turned and left the room. Belana stole a glance in his direction as she and Eli walked across the room to their table. It was good that he had decided to leave. Now she could concentrate, without being distracted, on how to tell Eli she couldn't see him anymore.

Eli held her chair out for her and after she was seated, he bent his long legs and sat down beside her. He was glad the other couples were on the dance floor. What he had to say was best said in private. He searched her eyes. "Belana, there's something I need to tell you before another minute passes. I lied about…"

"Being twenty-five?" Belana said, smiling at him.

He lowered his eyes, embarrassed. "I'm sorry. I didn't think you'd go out with me if you knew I was only twenty-two."

It occurred to Belana that Eli had been watching her and Nick so closely while they'd been dancing because he feared Nick would reveal his true age. Which he had done.

Belana laughed softly. "Six years isn't such a big deal. But I would have preferred the truth." She reached over and placed a hand atop his. "That being said, I also have a confession to make."

"You do?" said Eli, his thick brows arching in surprise.

"Nick and I aren't strangers," she said, coming out with it.

"But you acted as if you didn't know each other!" Eli exclaimed, clearly not pleased with this news. He sat frowning at her, looking petulant and put upon.

"He was following my cues," Belana explained, offering him an appealing smile. "I didn't want to explain in front of everyone that I used to date your agent."

Eli's frown deepened. "Nick's your ex-boyfriend?"

"We dated about two months and then there was a misunderstanding and I told him I didn't want to see him anymore," Belana explained. "But that's not the important part. After seeing Nick tonight, I realize breaking up with him was a boneheaded decision on my part. I was unfair to him. He tried to make it up to me, but I stubbornly refused to return his calls."

Eli put a hand to his forehead as if he'd developed a migraine after hearing her confession. "I don't know how Catholic priests listen to this kind of stuff year in and year out," he joked.

Belana was pleased he was taking this so well. It

was a good sign that he could crack a joke after what she'd told him. In essence, their first date would be their last.

"This is so weird," Eli said, looking at her with a woebegone expression in his dark eyes. "You're breaking my heart. And Nick! Nick has never been anything but honest with me. He asked you to dance to get you alone, didn't he?"

Belana nodded. "He wanted to have his say because eight months ago, I never let him explain himself. Now, though, I know why he did what he did, and I know why I haven't been able to put him out of my mind and move on. You're the first guy I've gone out with since Nick and I stopped seeing each other."

"Oh, damn," moaned Eli. "You're about to tell me goodbye, aren't you?"

Belana gently squeezed his hand. "I'm sorry, Eli. I can't date you knowing how I feel about Nick."

"Has he given you hope?" Eli asked.

"No, we haven't really talked, just admitted to each other that we both messed up. But I'm hoping he'll forgive me."

Eli smiled. "What could you have done that would require forgiveness?" He bent his head and kissed her knuckles. Sighing with resignation, he rose and pulled her up with him. "That was a rhetorical question. I guess you want to run after him and see if you can still catch him?"

Belana's heart raced at the notion. Had Nick had time to leave the St. Regis yet?

"If you don't mind," she said. "You're my date. If you want me to stay until the end of the evening, I'm yours until then."

"Yes, but you're not really mine," said Eli. "Your heart belongs to Nick." He smiled ruefully. "Go, Belana." He started to say, *go with my blessings,* but thought he would sound too much like that Catholic priest he'd mentioned earlier.

Belana grabbed her clutch and tiptoed to kiss Eli's cheek. "You're a great guy, Eli Braithwaite."

"And yet I'm the one going home alone," Eli joked.

Hurrying away, Belana paused at the exit to blow him a kiss. Eli pretended to catch it as he watched her turn and practically run out of the room. After she had disappeared around the corner, he reached into his jacket pocket and retrieved his cell phone. Disappointed though he was, he knew when to call it a day. But he still had a few choice words for Nicolas Reed.

Nick's number was programmed into his cell phone. He pressed a button and Nick's cell phone began ringing.

Nick picked up on the third ring. "Eli," Nick answered, his tone sounding rather worried to Eli's ears. Or maybe Eli just wanted him to sound nervous about a phone call from him, especially since he'd stolen his date right out from under his nose!

"Are you still in the hotel?" Eli asked.

"Yes, I'm downstairs in the bar having a drink," said Nick a bit hesitantly. "Why?"

"I should come down there and knock you out," Eli

said through clenched teeth. "Belana told me about you two, and then she said she couldn't see me anymore."

"She did?" Nick asked with a break in his voice. Eli thought Nick might have been trying to keep his tone neutral when what he really wanted to do was shout for joy.

"That's right," Eli continued angrily. "I hope you're happy, you woman-stealing son of a b…"

"Eli!" Nick admonished. "Your mother, the pastor, would be appalled at your language."

Eli laughed. "My mother's not here. I never even got the chance to kiss Belana. I'm sure that's an unforgettable experience."

"It is," Nick agreed.

"I thought so!" Eli said regrettably. "You don't have to sound so smug about it."

"I didn't mean for any of this to happen, Eli. I didn't know Belana would be here tonight. If I had, I might not have shown up," Nick said sincerely.

"But you did, and dateless. If you'd brought a date, like any normal guy, she would've kept you in line and not allowed fate to step in and give you another chance with my dream girl!"

"Now you're laying it on a little thick," Nick accused his young friend. "You're actually okay with this, aren't you, Eli?"

Nick tried to keep the laughter out of his voice, but didn't succeed. It had occurred to him that Eli Braithwaite was used to women falling all over him, doing anything to get the attention of the multimillionaire ballplayer. This might be a minor blow to his ego, but he was twenty-two; he would bounce back.

"Okay, you got me," admitted Eli, laughing. "But I had you going there for a minute. By the way, don't go anywhere because Belana's on her way downstairs to find you."

"I'm not going anywhere," Nick promised. "Thanks for being so understanding about this. A lesser man wouldn't have been."

"My pastor mother taught me well," said Eli. "Talk to you later."

"All right, man, you take care," said Nick, and closed his cell phone. In the St. Regis's premier bar, the King Cole Bar, he sat in front of the Maxfield Parrish Art Nouveau mural, which was the centerpiece of the establishment. The huge mural which depicted King Cole and his court ran the length of the bar. Elegant gold-colored barstools blended in well with the polished wood of the mural's trim and the bar itself. He'd mentioned the King Cole earlier to Belana so he hoped she would try it first before looking for him elsewhere.

He sipped his Jack and Coke, trying not to be nervous. But he was. He'd rarely wanted anything to work out as badly as he wanted to fix this thing with Belana.

Chapter 4

"I'm such a dunce," Belana muttered to herself as she searched her cell phone for Nick's number. She was in the elevator on the way down to the lobby. A couple, obviously on a date if their stealing kisses were any indication, stood locked in each other's arms in one corner. Three businessmen in expensive suits were discussing where to go for a drink. Frustrated, she closed her cell phone and shoved it back in her bag. Why did she make it a habit of deleting the numbers of past boyfriends from her cell phone? Earlier, when she'd told Nick she had his number, she hadn't been lying. She had it. She just didn't have it on her. It was in her little black book at home in the top drawer of the nightstand next to her bed. That had been fine when she'd planned on phoning Nick after Eli took her home tonight. But now that she was trying to catch up with him before he left the St. Regis, that number at home wasn't doing her any good!

She glared at the descending numbers on the elevator's panel as if she could will them to move faster. When the display read Lobby, she impatiently paced in place until the door slid open. She was the first person out. Turning to her left, she searched the huge lobby. Guests were checking in at the desk, others were leisurely strolling through the lobby, impeccably dressed, obviously going out for a taste of the incomparable New York City nightlife.

She spun around, looking for any sign of Nick. No luck whatsoever. She hurried across the lobby to the entrance, went through the doors and underneath the awning. "Excuse me," she said to the uniformed doorman. "But did you see a tall, good-looking guy in a dark suit leave?"

The doorman, a Hispanic man in his mid-thirties with a thick black mustache and soulful brown eyes, smiled and said, "Could you be more specific? I see a lot of men in dark suits."

"He's African-American, around six-three, built like a linebacker and he has a neat beard, but no mustache like your lovely mustache." Flattery wouldn't hurt.

"No, I haven't seen anyone who fits that description," he told her matter-of-factly. "I've seen a lot of basketball players, but no football players."

"Thank you!" Belana called over her shoulder,

already retracing her steps and re-entering the lobby. She glanced at her watch. It was nearly eleven.

She didn't think Nick was a guest of the hotel, so he hadn't gone to a private room. If he hadn't left the premises, what amenities did the hotel have to offer visitors at this hour?

Then, it dawned on her: earlier, Nick had mentioned meeting him in the hotel's bar. Maybe he had gone in there for a drink before hailing a cab and heading home.

She turned and began walking in the direction of the King Cole Bar. She'd been there on a couple of occasions and had enjoyed the ambience.

Nick couldn't sit still any longer. He rose, put a twenty on the bar and started walking toward the exit. Here he was mentally willing Belana to find him when he should have been proactive and searching for her. It was true: your brain simply doesn't work right when love is in the equation. He paused in his steps as he made his way across the room. Where had that come from? Did he love Belana Whitaker?

He continued walking. He desired her more than he'd desired anyone else since Dawn's death. He was definitely intrigued by her. She was a complex woman and he was drawn to complex women. Strong women who had more going for them than just looks. They had only dated for two months but what he'd learned about her in those months had kept him interested for eight more. It hadn't been the memory of making love to her, either, because they hadn't made love yet. Now, perhaps, he would get to know her better and find out if what they felt for each other was worth fighting for.

He was almost at the entrance to the bar when Belana appeared in the doorway. He stopped walking. She spotted him and smiled. In a moment or two, they were standing in front of each other. "You remembered," he said as he reached for her hand.

She took it and let him lead her back to the bar. He held on to her hand until she was seated on one of the barstools. "Finally," she said, smiling broadly. "I searched everywhere I could think of. I even went outside and spoke to the doorman before I remembered you'd mentioned meeting you here. Sorry, my brain's not firing on all cylinders tonight."

They were looking into each other's eyes and didn't notice the bartender until he cleared his throat. "What can I get you?" he asked, smiling patiently.

"Belana?" asked Nick.

"I'd just like a mineral water with lime," Belana said to the bartender. In a lower voice, to Nick, she said, "I've already consumed my limit at the fundraiser."

Nick, not needing anything more intoxicating than her presence, said to the bartender, "Same for me."

The bartender left to prepare their drinks.

Nick's dark brown eyes raked over her lovely face. She had large whiskey-colored eyes whose expression right now was so sultry he was getting aroused. His gaze traveled to her pert nose, and full, heart-shaped mouth, down to her swan-like neck and that lovely hint of cleavage. Belana felt herself melting under his intense scrutiny. But she didn't want it to end. No one had looked at her like this…ever! Or perhaps she had not been as receptive to the lascivious stares of other men as she was to Nick's. Whichever reason, she was so turned on, her nipples were hard and they weren't the only body parts that were swelling in anticipation of sexual release.

She took a deep breath. She needed to talk seriously to Nick. She crossed her legs, but that only intensified the arousal between them. She uncrossed them and primly closed them. The bartender returned with their drinks and quickly made himself scarce again. They murmured their thanks.

Belana took a sip of her mineral water with lime and cleared her throat. She hated to break this lovely spell, but Nick deserved to know whom he might be getting involved with. That is, if he didn't walk out of her life forever after she'd had her say.

She wanted to capture the way he was looking at her right now in her mind's eye and make it an indelible memory of this night. His head was cocked to the side as he drank her in with his eyes. Although the bar was full of people, she felt alone with him. She felt like she was the center of his world. He definitely was the center of hers right now.

She leaned over and kissed him softly on the lips. Nick smiled against her mouth and pressed more firmly, but not aggressively so. Her lips parted and the kiss deepened. Tongues tasted, but did not plunder. They soon parted and continued to smile at one another.

"You're as sweet as I remembered," Nick said.

"So are you," she returned with a barely audible sigh. After a deep breath she began to talk. "I told you that even though I was angry about your dating someone else while we were seeing each other, I was also relieved."

"Yeah, that puzzled me," said Nick.

Belana made sure she maintained eye contact as she continued. "When we were dating I was locked into this belief that like my mother, I couldn't commit to a lasting relationship. To explain, I have to tell you about my family."

Nick nodded in agreement. They hadn't talked much about each other's families during their time together. They were just getting to know each other when the incident that broke them up happened.

"My mother divorced my father and abandoned my brother and me when I was barely two," Belana stated with no emotion. She believed that by this time in her life all of the emotions connected with her mother had long been wrung out of her. "I didn't see her again until I was ten when she decided to come to one of my dance recitals. I didn't even recognize her. My father had shown us pictures of her over the years, but pictures never did her justice."

"She's quite a beauty, huh?" asked Nick softly.

"She *is* beautiful but that's not all. She's very striking in person, kind of intimidating even though she's only five-two. She's cold and distant, completely contained as if control is the most important thing to her."

Nick didn't say anything, but his brows rose questioningly. "Maybe you've heard of her," Belana asked. "Mari Tautou?"

"Mari Tautou, the dancer?" Nick asked, sounding astonished. He only knew of her because of the few posters of female dancers his daughter had on her bedroom wall, Mari Tautou was prominently displayed. "My daughter is into ballet. She's got more posters of your mother on her wall than any other dancer."

"Many little ballerinas grow up wanting to be just like her," Belana said sadly. "I did."

Nick reached over and grasped her hand, squeezing it reassuringly. "I'm sorry she wasn't a better mother to you and your brother."

"Most of the time, I didn't even think about her. My dad was great. Erik and I never lacked for love. It was only times when the other kids at school had their mothers with them that I missed her. That I felt as if I were somehow unlovable because no mother combed my hair at night or took me shopping. Any number of things a mother does. Subconsciously, I really *did* miss her, though. I was drawn to dancing. Maybe I thought that if I was good at it she would come back and be my mother. But when she finally did come back she had only one thing to say to me." Her eyes began to tear up as the memory burned brightly. After her performance in the recital, this pretty woman in a white dress had walked up to her backstage. She had taken her small chin in her hand, tilted her head up so that she was looking her squarely in the eyes and said in a well-modulated voice, "You have the makings of a fine dancer. But you must work on your positioning, and you need more stamina. Running will give it to you, so run, little one, run!"

"She told me I needed to start running," Belana told Nick, "for stamina. After that she simply turned and left. My father walked backstage just before she left and the two of them stared at one another for a moment. He was frozen in shock. She smiled at him as if she pitied him. I remember that distinctly, how she looked at him. My father was my hero and I wanted to run after her and hit her for looking at him that way. And I would have but when I ran past my father, he grabbed my arm. 'Baby,' he said, pulling me into his arms for a hug, 'you were wonderful up there. The best Sugar Plum Fairy I ever saw.' And we never talked about it. It was as if she was an apparition. I think it hurt him too much to talk about her." She breathed deeply and exhaled. "Which brings me to the reason we're having this discussion," she said. "When I started dating I noticed that whenever a guy began getting serious about me, I would make up an excuse to stop seeing him. Worse, if *I* started to feel something for the guy, that inevitably meant he had to go."

"Because you believed that since you had inherited your mother's love of dance, you had also inherited her lack of commitment," Nick guessed.

"Yes, and because I saw how badly she'd hurt my father," Belana told him. "He didn't recover for years. He threw himself into his work and into raising me and Erik. It wasn't until around three years ago that he found happiness with another woman."

"That's an awful lot of responsibility for a young girl to shoulder," said Nick, looking into her eyes. "Taking on your mother's sins, saving unsuspecting men from the same fate as your father, while your happiness got put on the back burner."

Belana looked surprised. "You don't think I'm neurotic?"

"We're all a little neurotic, Belana. I'm a mess trying to raise my daughter without her mother. I feel guilty all the time because she's living with her grandmother but would rather be living with me. But I know with my schedule, she's better off with my mother. Family makes us nuts sometimes. Your mother sounds especially cold-blooded, but your father, on the other hand, sounds like a really great guy."

"He is," Belana immediately said, smiling.

"Then forget about your mother. One good parent is a lot more than some people get." Peering into her eyes, he smiled warmly. "What matters is, you recognized why you were running away from your emotions. And now you're ready to stand and face them."

"I am," Belana confirmed, smiling back at him. This was going better than she'd imagined it would. "Then you forgive me?"

"I do," said Nick. "Do you forgive me for using bad judgment in the first place and seeing someone else?"

"Like I've already told you," said Belana, "you didn't

do anything wrong. I had no right to expect you to be faithful to me when I was just looking for a way to get rid of you."

Nick winced. "It doesn't sound nice when you put it that way."

"It wasn't nice," Belana said. "In my effort to avoid being like my mother, I treated you cruelly, and I'm sorry about it."

Nick looked deeply into her eyes. "You're doing all this confessing, offering yourself up for judgment, and I haven't told you much about myself. Maybe my shortcomings will warn *you* off."

"What shortcomings?" asked Belana skeptically. "You mean your parenting difficulties? No parent is perfect. Most of them are winging it from day to day."

"No, not that," Nick replied. "I know I'm doing the best I can by Nona…"

"What did you say?" Belana asked, shocked.

"I know I'm doing the best…"

"No, your daughter's name," Belana clarified.

"It's Nona," said Nick, looking askance.

"Your mother's Mrs. Yvonne Reed?" Again, Belana's tone was rife with shock.

"How did you know that?"

"This is getting spooky," Belana said, staring at him now. "I've been mentoring Nona for at least six months. She's a good dancer, Nick. We met when I spoke at a community center in Harlem. She approached me and asked me to come to her dance class. I did, and the rest is history!"

"This *is* weird," Nick said, shaking his head in disbelief. "She holds so much inside these days, as if her life is a big secret for me to figure out." He sighed with regret. "She never once mentioned your name."

"She's a teenager," Belana said on Nona's behalf. "I went through a rebellious phase, and I adore my father. I'm sure Nona adores you, too."

"Sometimes I wonder," Nick said truthfully. He smiled again and recaptured her hand. "But I was about to confess something to you."

"I'm listening."

"I was guarding my heart when we met, too," Nick said. "I loved my wife, Dawn. When she died I thought I would die of heartbreak, but I kept going for Nona. I didn't date for years after she died, and when I started dating again no one could measure up to her. I know that, realistically, I've met some great women. But I couldn't see myself opening my heart to anyone. One part of me felt as if I were being unfaithful to Dawn. Another was afraid of loving anyone half as much as I loved Dawn and then losing her, too. I couldn't take that. Then I met you and realized you were the one. The one who could eventually make me love her as much as I had loved my wife. I panicked, and that's when I asked Roxanna out. That's the woman whom you saw me with that night. I was trying to distract myself from thinking too much of you."

Belana laughed. "We're a couple of nuts!"

"Certifiable," Nick agreed. He took a deep breath and exhaled. "That's what I wanted to explain to you. That you were the one who could either crush me or take me to a higher level."

Belana leaned in. "My vote goes to taking you to a higher level."

They kissed again. This time softly, tenderly and lingeringly. Afterward, Belana opened her eyes and looked into his. "There's only one thing left for me to leave you with."

"Leave me?" Nick asked incredulously. "We've just gotten back together."

Belana smiled sadly. "I'm afraid I'm going to Greece tomorrow. My best friends and I go on vacation together every two years. We live so far apart. It's the only time we get to spend together anymore, except for family weddings, funerals and so forth. I wouldn't go, but it's all planned. I'll be back next Saturday evening, though, hopefully no later than nine."

Nick reluctantly nodded as if he understood. "Okay, well, what was the only thing you had to leave me to ponder over while you're gone?"

"My father is John Whitaker," she announced without preamble.

"John Whitaker, the man who saves entire towns?" Nick cried, his voice squeaking a bit.

"Well, I wouldn't say that," Belana said modestly.

"He goes in, buys faltering businesses, makes them work again, and saves hundreds of jobs. Yes, in this economy, I would say he saves towns." He laughed. "I'm talking to John Whitaker's daughter?"

"Now see, that's why I thought I should go ahead and break it to you," Belana said knowingly. "It takes some folks a little time to adjust and come to the conclusion that John Whitaker is just a man. He really is just a man. He's kind of shy. He loves his family and he cares for the people who work for him. It was a twist of fate, and a whole lot of hard work, that made him so successful."

Nick truly was impressed. He had admired Belana's father for years. He had even been inspired by John Whitaker's example when he had decided to become a sports agent shortly after he passed the bar exam. He'd read somewhere that Whitaker was honest to a fault. He had built his empire not by stepping on the backs of others, but by hard work and determination and by treating everyone with respect. Nick vowed he would never try to take advantage of his clients and would always be honest with them. He had kept that vow to this day.

"Okay," he said, calmer now. "Is there anything else I need to chew on while you're sunning yourself in Greece?"

"Ours is a blended family," Belana explained. "The friends I'm going to Greece with are Patrice Sutton-McKenna and Elle Jones-Corelli. We've been friends for about eleven years."

"Wait a minute, 'the' Patrice Sutton-McKenna, the actress who married T. K. McKenna?"

"Yeah," Belana said nonchalantly. She knew he would calm down eventually. "Anyway, since we three were friends, we started introducing our families to each other and Elle's mother and my father fell in love and got married. Now Elle is my stepsister. And her mother, Isobel, is the mother I never had. I just love her."

"Any more bombs to drop?" Nick asked hoarsely.

Belana smiled sweetly. She leaned over and kissed him on his chin, right over that adorable cleft in it. "No, that's it." She looked him intently in the eyes. "I know it's a lot to think about, but since we ended on a bad note eight months ago, I wanted you to know what baggage I brought with me so we could begin anew, with everything out in the open. Think on it, and when I return from Greece you can call me and tell me where we go from here."

She drank a big swallow from her glass of mineral water and lime and set the glass back down. "I'd better go now," she said regrettably. "I have an early flight out."

Nick paid the bill and got up, offering her a hand down from the bar stool.

As they walked arm in arm toward the exit, Belana laughed shortly and said, "This has been an interesting night, huh?"

"Considering that I only planned to show my face at a fundraiser and go home and have an early night, yes, it has been," Nick agreed.

Outside, he hailed a taxi. One from a queue waiting

in front of the St. Regis screeched to a halt in front of them in a matter of seconds. "I'll see you home," Nick said. Belana went into his arms. They were standing so close that their mouths were only inches apart. Belana tilted her head back and kissed him on the chin. "The way I'm feeling right now, you'd end up spending the night and I think we should take things slower."

Nick, who was aroused, agreed. He felt as if they'd already wasted eight months, though. However, anything worth having was worth waiting for. He bent his head and kissed her full on the mouth. Belana moaned softly and surrendered to his passion, his strength. They made it count, that kiss. It was meant to last them seven days. Seven days without one another. Seven days to dream of each other. Seven days to layer sexual tension on top of sexual tension.

When he put her in the cab and closed the door after her, she looked up at him longingly, thinking perhaps she had been too hasty in deciding not to spend the night in his arms. Nick handed the cabbie two bills, which would cover the fare and then some, and said, "Take care of her." Then he stepped back from the curb and watched the taxi pull away with Belana looking back at him.

What a night.

Chapter 5

Two days later, after an overnight stay in London, Belana was on a ferry en route to Mykonos in the Cyclades, a group of islands in the Aegean Sea. She stood at the railing, the breeze in her hair, the morning sun warm on her exposed skin. She felt a little weary from traveling, but buoyant nonetheless. Images of Nick kept playing in her mind's eye, making her smile. Innocent pictures because they had never made love. She didn't even have sexy memories to console her now that she was half a world away. But she felt confident that when she got back to New York his answer to whether or not they should be together would be yes. She wanted him in her life. She just hoped that laying everything on him at once hadn't been too much for him to take. Even the strongest of men were sometimes intimidated by wealth and celebrity. But should she be penalized because of who she was? For years she had wrestled with that question. Having a substantial amount of money and trying to explain to someone who didn't that you were just like them was a hard sell. Even her friends Elle and Patrice hadn't cut her any slack when they were at school. They would often be struggling to come up with money for entertainment or new clothes and other incidentals when all she had to do was inform her father she needed something and she got it. She was generous with her belongings, but after a while her friends grew irritated with her generosity, their pride wounded because they could rarely return her kindness with gifts of their own. Belana was patient, though, and the three soon learned how to accept each other as they were. It was a balancing act that they still practiced, loving one another, faults and all.

Belana had never been in a long-term relationship with a man before, though. She certainly didn't discuss how much money she had with men who were just passing through, which was why she'd only recently told Nick about her family.

Her thoughts were interrupted as the ferry drew closer to the dock. She thought she spied Elle and Patrice standing on the wooden planks, Elle's two-year-old, nearly three-year-old daughter, Ariana, whom everyone called Ari, in Elle's arms. Elle pointed at the ferry and Ari began waving at Belana. Belana vigorously waved back with a wide grin.

When the passengers formed a line to begin disembarking, Belana got in line, holding her suitcase in one hand and her big bag slung over her other shoulder. She had learned to pack light over the years. Trains, ferries and other modes of transportation in Europe rarely had room to stash huge suitcases so you were better off with smaller cases. Plus, who needed to be lugging around lots of bags when you were on vacation?

The three friends ran to embrace one another. Belana had seen Elle and Patrice only three months ago when they'd come to the opening of Swan Lake, but they greeted each other as if they hadn't seen each other in years.

Belana took Ari from her mother's arms and kissed her chubby cheeks. "You get more adorable every time I see you!" she exclaimed. Which was true. Ari had her mother's thick black hair and large brown eyes, and her skin color was somewhere between her mother's medium reddish brown and her father's golden brown. Sometimes Belana thought she looked more like her mother but recently she'd begun to look more like her father, Dominic. "My God, Elle, when did she start scowling like the Maestro?" Belana joked. Elle's husband was an operatic composer and he scowled when he was deep in thought.

"She's just squinting in the sun," Elle said, reclaiming her daughter and helping her on with her sunglasses, which Ari hated and promptly removed. "Ari, these are to protect your eyes from UV rays."

Ari asked her mother what UV rays were in Italian. Elle explained in Italian. Ari still stubbornly refused to wear the sunglasses.

Patrice picked up Belana's suitcase and they began walking in the direction of town where the driver they had hired to bring them to the docks was waiting at the car to take them back to the resort. Belana soaked up her surroundings: a marriage of old and new, the town was home to many blindingly white buildings. Against the backdrop of a deep blue sky and the crystal clear, blue waters of the Aegean, the whole effect was breathtakingly beautiful.

The people on the street were a mix of locals and tourists. Most of the locals were attired in contemporary fashions like their visitors, however, every now and then Belana spotted a few who kept the old ways, wearing simple peasant clothing and leading a donkey burdened with a heavy load.

"I can see why ancient Greeks invented the gods," Belana said. "This place is so gorgeous it inspires a belief in the supernatural."

"Isn't it?" asked Patrice, who had chosen the location. "And don't say anything to anger the gods while we're here, please. We'd like to relax and not worry about thunderbolts from out of the blue."

They laughed.

"So, Belana," said Elle, after they had control of their giggles, "Patrice tells me you're dating a boy of twenty-five."

"Actually, he's twenty-two and we're not seeing each other anymore," Belana informed them.

"What happened?" asked Patrice. "You didn't call me like I asked you to, so I've been wondering."

"One weird but wonderful thing after another," Belana began. She went on to tell them about running into Nick, whom they already knew of because she had told them how she felt she had foolishly let a good man get away. When she finished, her friends were laughing uproariously.

"I'm surprised you didn't tell him you snore," said Patrice, referring to the fact that Belana had forewarned Nick about everything that might work to keep them apart.

"I do *not* snore!" Belana denied.

"Yes, you do," said Elle, who had been Belana's roommate at one time. "For a tiny person, you snore like a Sumo wrestler."

"A buzz saw," Patrice interjected.

"You should probably ask your doctor to check your uvula, that's usually the culprit that causes the problem. You're definitely not overweight," said Elle helpfully.

Belana grimaced. "You're both exaggerating. Don't tell me that when I have the potential of sleeping with a man again after my longest dry period ever that I have a snoring problem!"

"Okay," Elle conceded, moving Ari onto her opposite hip. "I might have gone overboard. And I don't agree with Patty. I don't think you sound like a buzz saw. It sounds more like an outboard motor on a very small boat. Putt, putt, putt…you do this funny thing with your lips that's kind of like a raspberry but with a prolonged note." She demonstrated and Ari mimicked her.

Ari so enjoyed the raspberry sound that she continued doing it all the way to the car, driving her mother to distraction.

"That's what you get for ridiculing me," Belana crowed once they were comfortably seated in the air-conditioned car. The driver, a young Greek named Stavros, helped the ladies into the car, stowed Belana's suitcase in the trunk, after which he got back behind the wheel. He then greeted Belana with, *"Kalimera."*

"That means good morning," Patrice informed Belana.

"Kalimera," Belana said, liking the way the lilting words tripped off her tongue.

Even though he greeted newcomers with his native language, Stavros spoke English. "Where to, ladies?" he asked, turning around to peer at them with a smile crinkling his deeply tanned face.

"Back to the resort, please," Patrice spoke up.

"Consider it done," he said pleasantly, turning around and putting the car in gear. As they drove, Belana noticed that there were many men strolling through the town holding hands and generally behaving like couples.

"What is this town?" she whispered to Patrice sitting beside her. "The gay capital of Greece?"

Patrice laughed quietly. "Elle and I wondered about that, too, but, no. The town seems to be a mecca for gay couples, though. They've been celebrating what they call The International Gay Festival for the past week. Just this morning we were invited to a party tonight."

"Yeah, by Jon and John," said Elle, smiling. "They're supposed to be getting married on the Isle of Delos tomorrow."

"Is gay marriage legal in Greece?" Belana asked.

"No, it's not," Patrice replied. "According to John and Jon some judges have been willing to overlook the law and perform the ceremony anyway. I guess it's the romantic setting of Delos that the happy couple wants to experience. Delos is said to be a spiritual epicenter, kind of like Sedona, Arizona."

"The god Apollo was born on Delos according to Greek mythology," Elle put in.

"Then it must be good luck to get married there," Belana concluded.

"Yeah," said Patrice. She laughed. "I wonder if Vegas will be looked at in that way a thousand years from now."

She and her husband, T.K., had eloped to Vegas. However, they'd had a church wedding in her hometown of Albuquerque, New Mexico, a few weeks later. Their parents hadn't been happy that no one in either family had been present when they'd wed in Vegas.

"Who knows?" asked Belana lightly. "The only thing I know is none of us will be around to see it."

They laughed and settled back in their seats as Stavros drove them through the narrow streets of the quaint little town. Elle cuddled Ari, who had grown quiet in her arms, and softly sang something to her in Italian.

"Is that her default language?" Belana asked.

"Not surprisingly, it is," said Elle. "She speaks English, but everyone around her speaks Italian so she naturally speaks it, too. She adores her little cousins and whatever they do, she mimics."

"I think it's great that she's growing up bilingual," Belana said, rubbing her niece's back. "She's way ahead of her auntie. I'm happy to be able to speak one language."

"How'd closing night go?" Patrice asked Belana, changing the subject. The most practical minded of the trio, she was always concerned about how their careers were going.

"It was a solid performance," Belana told her. "I felt pretty strong considering the number of performances we did per week. I'm looking forward to the new season. I'm determined to make what might possibly be my last year my best year."

"You're not thinking of quitting before thirty?" Patrice asked, her voice rising in surprise. "Not you who aspired to last as long as… What's the name of that ballerina who retired from New York City Repertory Dance Theatre a few years ago?"

"Kyra Nichols," Belana said. "She retired after thirty years." She sighed. "What she did was amazing, but I don't think I'm going to last that long. I've been dancing for over twenty years already, only professionally for about ten, but I can already recognize the signs."

"Signs?" asked Elle. Ari had gone to sleep, so she had practically whispered the word.

"Signs that my body is sending me," Belana explained. "For one thing, I don't recover from a long performance as quickly as I used to. It's harder to get up in the morning. I used to be up at the crack of dawn ready to endure a rigorous two-hour dance class. Plus, my chiropractor says my spine isn't taking the abuse as well as it used to. I had a bulging disc on my sciatic nerve. Luckily my doctor caught it before it got really bad."

"Belana, why didn't you tell us?" Patrice cried, worried about her friend's health now.

"I didn't want to bother you," Belana said, sounding unconcerned. "It's not a chronic problem and it's treatable. I had injections and it went away."

"Didn't that hurt?" Elle whispered.

"I'm not afraid of needles," Belana replied. She sighed deeply. "The important thing is I'm fine. I think I have two more great years in me and want to dance some of the roles I've longed to dance like Aurora in *Sleeping Beauty* and Titania in Balanchine's *A Midsummer Night's Dream*. City Ballet is putting on *Dream* next season and I will dance Titania or die trying."

"A girl has to have goals," said Patrice teasingly. She knew that Belana would have to compete against some of the finest dancers in her company for such a coveted role. "I'm keeping my fingers crossed for you."

"Besides," Belana said, continuing with the reasons

she was thinking of quitting in two years, "I want to get married and have babies. When I do get married and have children I'd like to be a full-time wife and mother. I know dancers who do it all, but not without sacrifice. I feel like the only reasons a dancer keeps dancing beyond the point when her body's telling her to quit is because she's either financially in need or she craves the spotlight too much to quit. Like boxers who go back into the ring after retiring, or other athletes who simply can't stay retired and keep coming back in one form or another."

Elle laughed softly. "Michael Jordan, for example, who missed the game so much he wound up buying a team."

"Or George Foreman who came back in his forties," said Patrice. "I know what you mean," she said to Belana. "You want to bow out gracefully."

"Yes," said Belana. "And quit while my body can still push out a couple of babies."

"I love babies," said Stavros.

The three friends laughed. They had forgotten they were not alone. But that's how it was with them when they were together—totally engrossed in one another.

Later, they had lunch on the patio of their suite. Ari was asleep in her mother's bedroom and Elle had the baby monitor close by so she could hear her when she woke.

"Now that I have you two together," Belana said to Elle and Patrice, "I can ask you. Is marriage what you thought it would be?" She wore a smirk, which Elle and Patrice knew preceded ribbing.

The dynamics of their relationship had changed somewhat with their marital status. Belana used to be the bossy one, the one who gave advice even when it wasn't needed. She was older than Elle and Patrice by a few months, and used to rub that in, too. They all knew that life wasn't a race and it didn't matter which of them got married first or had a baby first. However, sometimes a bit of comparing lives *was* cathartic.

"No, it isn't," Patrice said frankly. She smiled. "It's better!"

"Come on," said Belana, disbelieving. "T.K.'s perfect? Is that what you're telling me?"

"Far from it," Patrice said. "He's all too human, which is what I love about him. Perfection is overrated. He's only perfect in the movies." Her eyes sparkled with laughter. "He doesn't want to be away from me for more than a week and, believe me, with our schedules, making sure we don't be apart longer than that is hard to do." Her short black hair was naturally curly and she had it shaped at the nape in a V. She ran her hand through it, remembering how her husband liked to run his hands through it. "Lately, all he talks about is having a baby."

"Are you?" asked Belana excitedly. "You've been married over a year and half, right?"

Patrice drank a bit of her water before answering. "I want to have a baby but my career is going so well now, it would set me back years if a project had to be postponed because of a pregnancy."

Elle, who had been silent until now, simply enjoying her meal, looked intently at Patrice, and said, "If you're looking for the most advantageous time to have a baby, it'll never come. Most of the parents I know didn't plan their children down to the minute, Patty. Look at me, I got pregnant and was going to leave Dominic rather than suffer the humiliation of begging him to marry me because I was pregnant. I wanted it all—love, marriage and a baby. I got love, a baby, and then the marriage. Life isn't neat, it's downright messy sometimes."

"Have you seen my husband?" Patrice cried. "He's built like, well, a Greek god! If I got pregnant I would be fat and grotesque. He works with beautiful women all the time, then to come home to *me* looking like a beached whale!"

Elle laughed. "I can't believe those words are coming out of your mouth." She looked at Belana, appealing to her for backup. Then she returned her attention to Patrice. "You're saying you don't trust T.K.?"

"Of course I trust T.K.," Patrice said, exasperated.

"Then you're just making excuses, Patty," Elle said. "I used to admire the fact that you were so ambitious, but I'm beginning to wonder if your ambition is hiding something else, like insecurity."

Patrice stared at Elle, shocked. "I'm not insecure, I just have a five-year plan, and having a baby doesn't come until the third year of marriage when I will be able to take a couple years off from work. I'll have ten films under my belt by then. Compared to T.K.'s thirty or so, that's not much, but at least I won't be forgotten while I'm gestating."

Elle couldn't control her laughter. Tears were streaming down her face she was laughing so hard. "Oh, Patty, now you're competing with one of the top box-office draws in the world? My, haven't we gotten egotistical!"

"Yeah," Belana agreed. "What's happened to you?"

Patrice felt like they were ganging up on her. She looked from Elle to Belana. "If you were in the business I'm in, you would understand. I have to maintain a certain level of success in Hollywood. Before I married T.K., nobody knew my name, or it felt like it. But suddenly I'm living in his world and they're saying things like I'm not worthy of him, and he could have chosen better. Things like that can *make* you insecure!"

She stopped with her mouth momentarily open in surprise by what she had just said. Elle had hit the nail on the head. She *was* insecure. "When did that happen?" she asked softly, more to herself than to her friends. "I swore I wouldn't let Hollywood get to me. I swore that T.K. and I would have a normal marriage based on love, and I've changed in spite of it." She looked at her friends with tears in her eyes.

She got up and went around the table to hug Elle. "Thank you, sis, you called it."

Elle got up and hugged her tightly. Belana joined them in a group hug.

"Problem identified, now we solve it," Elle said with determination.

For the next five days the friends shopped, swam in the sea, and went back to the resort to be massaged by muscular male massage therapists on open-roofed verandas with the sea breezes cooling their warm skin.

By the time they boarded the ferry to leave Mykonos they felt strengthened by the encouragement they'd given each other. And even more certain of the solidity of their friendship.

Belana arrived back in New York on Saturday evening. She took a taxi from the airport and when she got home, she dropped her bags on the foyer floor and immediately went to check her answering machine on the foyer table, hoping for a message from Nick. It had taken a great deal of restraint not to phone him from Greece, but she had been determined to wait. Now she was dying of curiosity.

She had plenty of messages from friends and acquaintances who weren't aware she would be out of town when they called. However none were from Nick.

Suddenly drained of energy, she walked slowly through the apartment and once in her bedroom began peeling off her clothes. Jeans, shirt, athletic shoes all ended up in a pile at the foot of her bed. Then she threw herself face down on to the queen-size bed.

"I scared him off," she muttered into her pillow.

Chapter 6

While Belana was in Greece Nick was extremely busy. He had to renegotiate a multimillion-dollar contract for one client, reminding management that he'd been indispensable to the team during the NBA finals this year. Then there was the twenty-one-year-old kid who was being courted by a beleaguered baseball team in Florida. Nick advised the kid not to take the job, but he was from Florida and had dreamed of playing for that particular team all his life. He naively felt he could singlehandedly turn the ball club around. Nick was at a loss trying to convince someone with that kind of faith in the team of his boyhood dreams to seek a position with a team that could offer him a more secure future.

The kid would not budge, so Nick had gotten him the best deal he could under the circumstances. He didn't feel particularly optimistic about the chances of the team's prospects improving, but in his years of following sports, stranger things had happened.

On the home front, he'd gone to church with his mother and Nona on Sunday. His mother had been delighted he could join them, but Nona, still miffed at him—that girl could really hold a grudge—pretty much ignored him.

Over dinner, she talked animatedly with his mother, mostly about dance. Nick felt like a third wheel. He had eaten his meal and watched her. She looked so much like Dawn. The same milk-chocolate toned skin and almond-shaped golden brown eyes. She had his black hair, though. Dawn's hair had been dark brown. She also had his chin. The cleft in it was exactly like his.

His daughter caught him looking at her across the table and frowned. "What's the matter?"

"Nothing's the matter," he'd said, smiling. "I was just thinking how much you look like your mom."

There was a hint of a smile at the corners of her mouth, but she beat it back down and sighed as if he were tiresome. "You say that all the time."

"Because it's true all the time," he countered, perhaps a bit too sharply.

His mother cleared her throat, something she did whenever she wanted to caution someone at her dinner table against bad behavior.

Nick took a deep breath and tried again. "How are your dance classes coming along?"

Nona looked at him with more than a little suspicion. "Why? You want to make sure I'm going when I should be going so that I'm not wasting your hard-earned money?"

"No, because I'm interested," he said. He wanted her to tell him about Belana mentoring her so that he could casually mention that he knew Belana. Then they would at least have that in common.

"Why are you interested all of a sudden?"

Nick put his cloth napkin in his plate, denoting he was finished eating. This time, though, he felt he was also finished trying to make nice with his stubborn daughter.

He regarded her with narrowed eyes. "Nona, let's make one thing perfectly clear. I am your father, and I'm interested in every aspect of your life whether you believe it or not. And I think it's time you stopped punishing me for doing what fathers the world over do for their children, provide for them!"

Nona jumped when he raised his voice toward the end of his speech.

Nick immediately regretted his tone. Why must she push his buttons?

Tears collected in the bottom rims of Nona's eyes. Her bottom lip stubbornly poked out and began to tremble slightly. Nick sighed. He hated when she tried to manipulate him with tears. It was what she fell back on when she thought she was losing an argument.

He smiled at her. "You're not three years old anymore. You're fifteen, a young woman. Be mature enough to deal with your father without the theatrics, please."

Nona blinked back tears. Her nose began to run. She picked up her napkin, dabbed at her eyes and wiped her nose. "I really don't have anything to say to you that you haven't already heard from Momma Yvonne. I'm getting good grades in school and I never miss a dance class. Your money is being well-spent. I'm trying to be a model daughter for a model father."

"Sarcasm," Nick said, "is lost on me." He grasped her wrist between strong fingers and said, "Look at me, Nona." She reluctantly met his eyes. "I'm all you have. Make the best of it. Now, since you won't share what's going on in your life, I'm going to share with you what's going on in mine. I've met someone."

Nona's brows rose in surprise. Her father didn't often mention women. She had begun to think he had lost interest in that kind of thing. But she supposed he wasn't old and decrepit yet at only thirty-three. He and her mom had been teenagers when she had been born. In some ways she admired him for not freaking out like she'd heard some guys did when they found out they were going to be fathers and leaving the girls to deal with it on their own. He had married her mother and both of them, with the support of their parents, had gone to college. Her mother had become a teacher and he'd eventually gotten his law degree.

Her gripe with him wasn't about his not supporting

her financially. It was about his spending time with her. Now, he was telling her he was interested in a woman. A woman who would take whatever time he had allotted for *her* out of his already busy schedule. That didn't seem fair to her.

"I'm happy for you," she said, her voice dripping with sarcasm.

"You really are not good at that," Nick told her, smiling. "Don't you want to know her name, and what she does for a living?"

"I'm not interested in your love life unless, of course, you're going to get married and start having babies. Then, I suppose I can come visit you and the stepmom parental unit and the new rug rats. I hope you have a girl. I always wanted a sister."

Nick winced. Maybe she was good at sarcasm after all.

Nona smiled smugly.

"We haven't discussed marriage," Nick said, keeping his tone purposefully light. "We have discussed you, though. She thinks you're a good dancer."

Nona stared at him, smug smile gone. "You're dating my dance teacher?" she screeched.

Nick laughed. "If your dance teacher is Belana Whitaker then, yes, I'm dating your dance teacher."

"Belana!" Nona cried. She removed her napkin from her lap and threw it on to her plate, which was still practically full. Glaring at her father, she said, with a great deal of skepticism in her tone, "Really? Where did you meet?"

Nick was happy to have finally gotten her undivided attention. "We go to the same chiropractor," he told his daughter. "She was leaving the elevator one day, the heel of her shoe got caught on loose carpeting and she went to fall and I caught her. It was very romantic, really."

Nona stared blankly. "She never mentioned knowing you," she said, stunned.

"That's because she didn't know you were my daughter," Nick explained. "We dated a couple of months then we broke up. I only met her again last night. She apparently started mentoring you after we broke up. She and I hadn't discussed family at length. She knew I had a daughter but not your name or how old you were. If you had ever mentioned my name to her she would have put two and two together but you didn't."

"You broke up?" Her eyes stretched in disbelief. "What could possess you to break up with Belana Whitaker? Are you insane?"

Going for full disclosure, Nick told her why they'd broken up.

"I don't believe you," Nona groaned. "You were dating a woman like Belana Whitaker and you actually asked someone else out? I'm rapidly losing respect for you, Daddy."

Nick smiled. She'd called him Daddy. It had been a long time since she'd done that. Usually whenever she referred to him it was in third person, as in: You're my father, so what? And as for respect, that was news to him. He'd had no idea she respected him.

He believed he'd told her enough, so he simply said, "I made a mistake."

"Duh, you think so?" said his sarcastic daughter.

Nick laughed. "All right, you got me."

Nona smiled. Then, as if she'd remembered she was at war with her father, the smile vanished. "You said you saw her again last night. You've made up, and everything?" she asked doubtfully.

"We've made up," Nick confirmed.

"Then why didn't you invite her to church with us this morning?"

"She's in Greece with friends," Nick explained, beginning to wish he had waited to bring up the subject of his and Belana's reconciliation until later. He saw now that Nona really admired Belana and the idea of his being in a relationship with her was rife with stress and worry for her. "It's not as if we knew we were going to get back together last night. It just happened."

His daughter shook her head in amazement. She rose. Looking at him with disgust, she said, "What if you break up again? Is she still going to be my mentor? I doubt it! If you mess this up for me, I'll never forgive you!"

She ran from the room.

Nick started to get up and follow her but his mother, who had listened quietly throughout their conversation, said, "Let her go, Nick. Give her some time by herself. She's just reacting. She hasn't had time to digest what you told her. She's smart. She'll realize that she has to share you with the world."

"She didn't sound as if it was me she didn't want to share," Nick said.

"I know it didn't, but it is," his mother assured him. "She's lashing out at you because now she believes she's going to get the short end of the stick since you have a special woman in your life. It'll all work out, dear. Be patient. Yes, she feels proprietary toward Belana because she admires her. She dreams of being just like her. But it's not Belana she's afraid of losing. It's you. Then, too, you have to remember that over the years you haven't gotten serious about anyone. You dated a couple of women for a while but nothing ever came of those relationships. Now you're singling out Belana. Nona is naturally going to rebel against the notion of anyone replacing her mother in her heart.

"She might have been too young when Dawn died to have a lot of memories of her, but she is fiercely loyal to her memory."

Nick hadn't thought about that. "You've obviously given this some thought," he said to his mother.

Yvonne smiled. "I've had plenty of time to think about what would happen if you ever got serious about someone. Dawn's been gone quite a few years, God rest her soul."

Nick closed his eyes in frustration. He had a lot to learn about being sensitive to his daughter's needs. He got up and walked to the far end of the table where his mother was sitting and hugged her in gratitude. "Don't know what I'd do without you," he said softly.

"Oh, you'd be okay," Yvonne told him, squeezing him back. "Let's have some sweet potato pie. The smell of it usually brings your daughter running."

Nona had indeed come downstairs when her grandmother had taken the freshly baked potato pie out of the oven, but she had eaten her slice in utter silence, not looking her father's way once.

All week, she had shut him out, not even taking his phone calls. Now it was Saturday evening, and Nick was weary of soul on one hand, and eager to see Belana again on the other.

As he sat in a taxi on the way to Belana's apartment building he tried to clear his mind and concentrate on just him and Belana. Didn't he deserve some happiness? He didn't know how other single parents managed to have a love life.

Since Belana had slept on the plane, she wasn't tired. She had lain on the bed only a few minutes lamenting her life, and the lack of a phone call from Nick. Then she'd gotten up and put on her dance togs and ballet shoes. She hadn't had a good workout since she'd left for Greece and to be truthful, the food had been a little too hard to resist. She intended to dance until she was washed in sweat.

She put three CDs in rotation in the CD player and turned the volume up loud but not loud enough to disturb her neighbors. One of the bedrooms in her two-bedroom apartment had been turned into a dance studio with a polished wooden floor, one wall entirely mirrored from ceiling to floor, and a ballet barre attached to that wall.

The first CD was a selection of her favorite opera solos. Luciano Pavarotti sang Nessun dorma as she warmed up with pliés at the barre. While she went through her positions her mind was on Nick. What had she done to chase him away? No, wait a minute. Why should she blame herself? If he couldn't handle a strong woman like her, it was totally on him! Wanting to be honest, she had leveled with him. She had thought that was a good thing. What was it that had made him think twice? Was it her father's wealth? He was intimidated by that? She hadn't thought Nick was the type of man who would let wealth and position intimidate him. She'd obviously been wrong. As she started doing tendus the buzzer sounded. Her building had a doorman, but after a certain time of night visitors were obliged to buzz residents for permission to enter the building.

Muttering to herself, she glanced at herself in the mirror before going over to the wall unit and pressing the button. She hadn't even broken a sweat yet. Who could be buzzing her after nine on a Saturday night? Most of her friends in town were thoughtful enough to phone before coming over. Only Ana and Erik just dropped in.

She cheered up a bit. She had thought she was fine alone but she would actually welcome company.

"Erik, Ana, is that you?" she said into the mouth-piece.

"No, it's Nick," came the familiar voice.

Her hear thudded with excitement. "Oh, my God, Nick. When I didn't have a message from you when I got back I thought you'd decided to pass."

He laughed. "That's not the sort of thing I'd do over the phone," he said. "May I come up?"

"Yeah, of course," she cried happily. She pressed the button that would allow him entrance into the building.

Belana ran to check her reflection in the mirror. She'd hastily braided her hair and it fell down her back. The white leotard, white leggings and pale pink ballet shoes were all clean. She looked at her teeth, and blew into her hand to test her breath, which wasn't bad, but in case kissing was going to be on the agenda, she wanted to be ready so she ran to the bathroom and quickly brushed. It would take Nick a good three minutes to get upstairs.

Her doorbell rang just as she was putting her toothbrush away. She breathed in and out, minty-fresh.

When she opened the door Nick was standing there in semicasual clothing of tan slacks and a brown, designer, short-sleeved polo shirt which admirably showed off his fit, muscular body, and a pair of brown leather loafers. He was immaculately groomed and smelled wonderful. She grabbed him by an arm and pulled him inside, breathing him in all at once.

"I hope the answer's yes, because as good as you smell it would be very cruel of you to tease me like this," she joked.

Nick grinned and pulled her into the crook of his arm with one hand. It was the welcome he was hoping for. She pressed her body against his, fitting nicely in his embrace, and turned her mouth up to his. He didn't have to be told what to do. He bent down and hungrily kissed her.

Belana closed her eyes and fell into the kiss. She had to tiptoe a bit because he was nearly a foot taller than she was since she wasn't wearing heels, but it was worth the effort.

To Nick, she had never tasted sweeter. Her plump lips were firm against his, and pliant. When she opened them, surrendering, inviting him in, her tongue met his in a teasing, tempting dance that incited him to arousal in a matter of seconds.

He raised his head long enough to say, "Door," because they were still standing in the doorway. Belana closed the door with her hip and quickly engaged the lock. Various deadbolts required attention, but they could wait.

Their eyes met. "If you had told me you didn't like leaving important messages on a machine I could have avoided the last few minutes of wondering what I'd done to chase you away," she said in a lightly accusing voice.

Nick produced a bouquet of pink roses from behind

his back. "I'm sorry, but if you remember, I wasn't thinking too clearly that night."

She accepted the roses and sniffed them appreciatively. They had a delicate, fresh scent that reminded her of the garden at her father's house in the Connecticut countryside. "Thank you."

She led him farther into the apartment. They stepped off the Berber carpeting runner that ran the length of the hardwood floor in the foyer, and onto the polished oak floor of the living room. Nick noticed what she was wearing. "You were dancing?"

"Warm-ups," she said. She gestured to the large, toffee-colored, cloth-upholstered sofa. "Have a seat while I run and put these in water."

"I'll come with you," said Nick. He was reluctant to let her out of his sight. She'd been gone a week, during which they'd had no contact whatsoever. They had a lot to say to one another.

Belana smiled and turned to go into the kitchen. "Sure," she said casually. "How is Nona and your mother?"

"They're fine," Nick said as they walked into the kitchen, a large room with Italian tile in off-white, burnished red cabinets and marble countertops. The stainless-steel appliances blended well with the decor.

In the kitchen, Belana went and removed the now-wilted roses Eli had given her from the vase on the kitchen table and dumped them in the trash receptacle underneath the sink. Nick was leaning with his back against the counter next to the sink, looking at her as she put clean water into the vase and began putting his roses into it.

There had been a space of two silent minutes that hung in the air while Belana had been doing this. She looked up into Nick's eyes. "What is it you're not saying?"

Nick, who had been content to simply watch her beautiful face for a while, smiled and rubbed his neatly shorn beard.

Belana laughed. "Not that."

"What?"

"You do that when you're trying to decide something," she said.

"I do?"

"Yes, you do. When we used to go to dinner you would do that when you were looking at the menu trying to decide what to order."

"I'd better pay attention to my nervous habits in the future," Nick said. "Otherwise you'll start to read me like a book."

Belana finished putting the roses into the vase. "Did you tell Nona about me?"

"You're a witch!"

"I'm a woman," Belana said with a gentle smile. She walked with the vase over to the kitchen table and set it in the middle of it. Nick followed her and when she turned around again, she turned right into his arms.

"I'd prefer to just talk about us tonight," he said as he lowered his head and kissed the side of her neck.

Belana knew it was bad then. Avoidance was something she was all too familiar with. She'd avoided facing up to the fact that she had wanted Nick after she'd tossed him aside. Now that she had been given another chance, she was not going to repeat the same mistakes.

"There will be no us if your daughter doesn't like me," Belana said. She searched his eyes. "Talk to me."

"Okay." Nick sighed. "I told her you and I were going to start seeing each other again and she got upset and yelled at me. She said if I messed up and it spoiled your relationship with her she'd never forgive me."

"Did you reassure her?" Belana wanted to know. She waited.

"She clammed up after that and hasn't spoken to me since," Nick admitted.

Belana hugged him. "Poor baby, you're really catching hell, aren't you?"

"I am," he said, his voice a soft whine against her neck.

Belana held him. She liked this, being the one to offer comfort. "Don't worry, I'll talk to her and let her know she doesn't have anything to worry about. Even if you decide to kick me to the curb, I will always be her friend."

Nick raised his head and met her gaze. "That's not funny."

She laughed nonetheless. "It's a little funny," Belana insisted. "What's even more funny is how you're letting

Nona's comments get to you because you feel guilty for having to let her live with her grandmother instead of you. You've either got to get rid of the guilt or let her move in with you. Why isn't she living with you again?"

"Because I work all the time and she's better off with her grandmother," said Nick. "I thought I explained that."

"You did, but, Nick, a lot of parents work too many hours, and their kids still live with them. Nona knows that and she's going to keep at you until you relent. Why don't you just relent and let her get a taste of what it's like to live with you. Then maybe she'll see your point of view. On the other hand, it might just work out for you both. She isn't a kid anymore. She doesn't really need a babysitter."

"I just feel better when I know she's with my mother when I'm out of town," Nick said in his defense.

"Then let her go to your mother's when you have to go on overnight or longer trips," Belana suggested. "Work with her."

Nick looked at her as if she might have struck on a good idea. "It's worth a try," he agreed. "I'll ask her."

Belana kissed his chin. "It's worth a try."

Nick returned her kiss, but to both cheeks, high on the cheekbones, to her forehead, making his way down to her rosebud-tinted mouth. "God, I missed you so much."

"I thought about you constantly," breathed Belana.

"I thought about the fact that I didn't even have the memory of our making love to tide me over."

"No," said Nick, "we never made love."

"Let's correct that mistake right now," Belana said in his ear as she snared his earlobe with the edge of her teeth, pulled it into her mouth and sucked on it.

Nick, who was already semihard, reached a full erection once his nerve endings got a load of her warm, wet tongue on his flesh. He picked her up. "Bedroom or couch?" he asked, his tone strangled.

"Bedroom," Belana said, "Second door on the right."

In the bedroom, Nick put Belana back on her feet and they kissed once more while their hands were busy undressing one another. When Belana was down to her lingerie, and he down to his boxer briefs, Nick paused. He'd just remembered that he hadn't brought condoms with him. For one thing, he hadn't planned on seducing Belana tonight, only to see her and give her his answer. He'd been sure she would want to wait a while longer before intimacy. Only a week ago, that had been her suggestion.

However, they *had* known one another for nearly a year.

Belana was looking up at him with a bemused expression. "I didn't think we'd end up in bed so I didn't bring condoms," he stated.

Belana smiled. "Top drawer of the nightstand," she told him. "I'd rather have them and not need them than need them and not have them."

"That makes sense," Nick said, and kissed her. He smiled to himself. He was nervous. Why was that? He was an experienced lover. He hadn't made love to anyone since he and Belana broke up, but that shouldn't affect his performance.

Belana softly moaned with pleasure. She hadn't even kissed anyone while she and Nick had been apart, let alone made love. She hoped he didn't think that just because she liked to be prepared for any contingency she was promiscuous. She could count all the lovers she'd had on one hand.

She broke off the kiss and peered up at him. "There's been no one since we broke up."

"For me, either," he told her, and nibbled on her bottom lip.

She was pleased by this and expressed her pleasure by pulling his boxer briefs past his hips and grasping his fully engorged penis firmly in her small hand. He was hot and long and thick. Their eyes met. She ran her hand along the veined length of him and enjoyed the soft moan of pleasure that issued from him.

Chapter 7

Nick had never been with a woman who knew how to use her body as well as Belana did. Not only was she extremely flexible but her stamina was beyond his expectations.

She turned him inside out. Taking all of him inside her and never ceasing to amaze him with her desire for more. She was astride him now, her hair wild and her skin aglow. Her nipples, like ripe berries, were hard and her full breasts bounced like breasts were supposed to as she rode him. He couldn't take his eyes off her. They had already used one condom and he'd had time to recover while she'd gone to the kitchen and come back with a bottle of chilled white wine. He wasn't a wine drinker and only took a sip. She'd drizzled a little between her breasts and he'd licked it off her. He had then acquired a taste for it, especially when it was coupled with the intoxicating taste of her warm skin. A few minutes later, he was hard again and she'd sat on him, allowing her sex to enfold him. She squeezed, making him convulse with intense pleasure. He began to feel as if he were in his own personal harem and Belana was his concubine making sure his every desire, expressed or unexpressed, were fulfilled.

She gasped as her second orgasm rocked her. She fell forward on to his chest and he held her until she came down from the precipice, then he pulled her more fully into his embrace and they rolled over on the bed, this time with him on top.

Belana spread her legs and smiled at him. His thrusts were long, hard and deep, and so satisfying. She bucked beneath him, heightening the sensation for him. He felt like he would explode, and then he did, his seed filling the tip of the condom to capacity.

He was washed in sweat, while Belana simply glowed. He smiled as he lay beside her on the bed. "I take it back, ballerinas *are* athletes."

Belana laughed. "You're a big man to admit it."

She sat up in bed. "I'm hungry." She peered at the clock on the nightstand. "It's only eleven. Want to go get something to eat?"

Nick did, so they got up, showered together and dressed, after which they went to a neighborhood pizzeria that stayed open past midnight and got a couple slices.

As they ate in the booth in the dimly lit dining room of the neighborhood mainstay, Nick marveled at the fact that a woman of Belana's background could enjoy a slice of pizza as much as any other girl from New York on a Saturday night.

He must have been looking at her too intently because Belana laughed at him, and said, "I can't get my feed on like I want to if you're going to be staring at me like that."

Nick laughed and looked away. "Better?" he asked.

While he was looking away, Belana took the last slice. "You can look now."

Nick laughed when he saw what she had done. "You deserve it. You really worked up an appetite."

Belana blushed prettily and devoured the pizza.

Later, Nick walked her home and before he kissed her good-night, he asked, "Would you like to go to church with us tomorrow morning?"

"I'd love to," she immediately answered.

Nick smiled. "You don't care where or with whom?"

"I'm assuming it's with Nona and your mother. As for where, Abyssinian Baptist Church in Harlem."

"Nona told you where she goes to church but nothing about her father?" Nick asked, clearly finding that irritating.

"We were talking about God and how He inspires the arts," Belana explained. "She said she feels very close to God at Abyssinian Baptist Church. She said it had to do with its history, a sense of all those people before her who made her existence possible. She's very deep, your daughter." She tiptoed and kissed his cheek. Looking into his eyes, she asked, "What time?"

"Service starts at eleven," Nick told her. "I'd better pick you up at 9:30. That'll give us time to go by and pick up Mom and Nona and still hopefully find a parking space."

"I'll be ready," Belana assured him.

Taking her face between his hands, Nick looked deeply into her honey brown depths. "Do you know what you're getting into? Dealing with a teenager is like walking a tightrope over the Grand Canyon without a harness."

Belana smiled encouragingly. "Let her give me her best shot, I'm ready for her."

Nick pulled her into his arms and hugged her tightly. He hoped so, because he was beginning to envision a future with Belana Whitaker.

On Sunday morning Odell Clark Place, which was formerly known as 138th Street, was crowded. Belana had done a little research after Nona had told her she attended Abyssinian Baptist Church with her grandmother. The church had been founded in 1808 when a group of black New Yorkers and Ethiopian seamen refused to be relegated to the segregated section in the First Baptist Church in the city of New York. After over two hundred years the Gothic and Tudor-style church stood as a testament to the strength and resilience of its members and was one of the most famous churches in New York City.

After she, Nick, Nona and Yvonne were seated on one of the pews in the front of the edifice, Belana glanced up at the stained-glass windows. They were beautiful depictions of Bible scenes. *Nona was right,* she decided, *you do feel closer to God in here.* She'd read that in 1937 this church had the largest congregation of any church in the United States with over 4000 members. At that time, Adam Clayton Powell, Jr. had been the pastor. Nat King Cole and his wife, Maria, had been married here and a host of other couples, famous and otherwise.

Belana turned her head to observe the long aisle down the middle. Yes, she could envision a bride walking down it, resplendent in white.

While Belana was admiring the building, Nona was observing her. *What am I going to do?* she wondered. *This thing with her and my dad won't last. She's a star, and he's...well, a lawyer. She thinks I don't know who she really is but I found her on Google. I know she's some kind of heiress. Her daddy has millions, probably billions. What is she doing with my dad? Sure, for a while they'll act like they're all in love and everything but when they wake up they'll realize they have nothing in common and I'll be the casualty. Dad will go back to ignoring me.* She glanced at her dad who was smiling at Belana. *Look at him. He looks like a fool. She's got him flying so high right now it's a wonder his nose isn't bleeding. But that's not the only thing that's gonna be bleeding in a little while because she's gonna rip his heart out. Why do grown-ups have to be so stupid? Don't they know their behavior affects us?*

The Rev. Dr. Calvin O. Butts, III began his sermon and everyone listened raptly. Nick, on Belana's left, held her hand, and Nona, on Belana's right, also held her hand. Belana wondered what, if anything, this meant. Were they simply trying to make her feel welcome or were they both claiming possession of her affections? She was sure she would find out sooner rather than later.

Yvonne, sitting on the other side of Nona, looked at her son and her granddaughter both holding on to Belana, and turned her eyes heavenward. She knew one thing: trouble was brewing. She could feel it in her bones. She just hoped that in whatever form it came they would all emerge the better for it. It had been her experience that trials and tribulations often had that effect. Nona and Nick had suffered enough already. Nona tried to appear tough, but she had a sensitive soul. As for Nick, Yvonne was happy he was in love after all this time. He hadn't told her he was in love, but she'd known him all his life. She knew. She thought he'd never feel for another woman what he'd felt for Dawn who had been his first love. He was the type of man who loved forever. Like his father, Nicolas, before him. *Her* Nick had been gone for nearly fifteen years. Yes, there had been enough pain in this family to last a lifetime.

With a smile on her pretty face, she turned her attention to the good reverend's sermon.

After the sermon concluded, nearly two hours later, the foursome stood up to join the other churchgoers in the center aisle but were waylaid by old friends who wanted to know who their visitor was. Introductions were made, and Belana found herself shaking hands with, and occasionally being hugged by, some of the friendliest people she'd met in a long time.

One woman, who appeared to be from Nick's mother's generation, hugged her to her ample bosom. "My name is Lyla Daly. I saw you dance two weeks ago," she said, grinning. She had such a chubby, rosy-cheeked brown face that her eyes nearly closed when she smiled broadly. "My, you're talented. You wouldn't know it to look at me now, but I used to dance. Arthur Mitchell, who was the first black dancer with the New York City Repertory Dance Theatre, said I had great promise. Unfortunately, I broke my right leg in three places in an accident when I was nineteen and that was the end of my career."

Belana was so touched, she hugged Lyla again. She imagined her spirit had been crushed, even worse than her leg, to have been denied the joy of dancing.

"That must have been devastating for you," she sympathized.

Lyla shrugged. "What can you do? I went on and discovered something I was even better at."

"I should say so!" Yvonne exclaimed. "She owns the best bakery in New York City."

Lyla kissed Yvonne's cheek for that compliment. "The check's in the mail," she joked, as if she paid her good friend to promote her business.

Nick, seeing a break in the long line of parishioners leaving said, "Let's get in line, shall we?" He ushered all four ladies in front of him and then stepped in the aisle himself. Belana was right in front of him, Nona in front of her, Lyla in front of Nona and Yvonne leading the way.

"The hard part about going to a popular church," he said in a soft voice to Belana, "is getting out of the church when the service is over."

They kept up a lively conversation all the way to the front steps of the church where Lyla hugged Yvonne goodbye and said to Belana, "It was lovely to meet you and I hope to see you again next Sunday."

"It was lovely to meet you, too," said Belana with a warm smile.

Lyla wiggled her fingers at them as she hurried off. Everyone waved goodbye.

After only a few minutes outside, the August heat started to make them perspire. The sun was high in the sky and lately the daytime temperatures had been in the low nineties.

"Ooh, it's hot out," Yvonne said as they walked down the street, heading to Nick's late-model SUV. Parking near the church was first come first served, and they had gotten there early enough to find a space across the street from the church.

As they crossed the street they looked like a family

of four in their Sunday best—Nick in a dark summer suit and tie with a crisp white shirt and black wingtips, and the ladies in light-colored summer skirt suits with heels, Belana and Yvonne in stylish hats, Nona with her short black hair in dreadlocks.

"Belana, you don't have to go straight home, do you?" asked Yvonne. "I was hoping you'd come to an early dinner." It was half past two in the afternoon by then.

Nick had only mentioned church last night, so Belana was surprised by the dinner invitation. Although, it would afford her the opportunity to talk with Nona, who had been generous with her affection since Nick had picked her and her grandmother up this morning, but hadn't said much. Plus, she was hungry.

Belana looked up at Nick to try to gauge his reaction to his mother's invitation. He smiled at her, and mouthed the word, "Please?"

"I'd love to, Mrs. Reed," Belana said.

"Wonderful," said Yvonne, pleased her invitation had been accepted.

"Yes!" cried Nona. "I'm dying to show you my collection."

"Your collection?" asked Belana, intrigued.

"My ballet memorabilia," Nona explained. "I've even got newspaper articles and magazine articles about you."

Belana had been interviewed in magazines about the arts a few times, and there had been stories about City Ballet that had appeared in New York area newspapers in which photos of her in mid-dance had appeared. "How sweet of you," she said to Nona.

Nona smiled up at her, obviously suffering from a bit of hero worship, which made Belana feel unworthy.

Nick got to the car first and rolled down all the windows, letting the hot air out, turned on the AC, and rolled the windows back up as the ladies got in. Once everyone was buckled up he pulled out into traffic and headed to his mother's house, which was less than a mile away. When the weather didn't induce heatstrokes his mother was known to walk to church on Sunday morning.

He had to drive slowly because of the congested traffic, both pedestrian and vehicle, so it took them fifteen minutes to get to the three-story brick row house between 138th and 139th Streets.

The first thing Belana noticed upon stepping into the well-kept, air-conditioned home was the lovely oak floors. Then she raised her eyes and took in the workmanship of the crown moldings and other architectural touches that must have been a part of the original structure. She was sure that renovations had been done over the years—it wouldn't look this fresh otherwise—but she felt as if she'd stepped into a 1920s Harlem row house like the famous houses on Strivers' Row where Harlem notables like musicians Eubie Blake and W. C. Handy, and actor Bill "Bojangles" Robinson once lived. "What a beautiful house," she exclaimed, which elicited a blush and a grateful smile from Yvonne.

She tried her best to keep up the house that had been in her husband's family for so many years.

"Thank you," she said to Belana. Everyone started removing their lightweight jackets or sweaters, and in the case of Yvonne and Belana, their hats, and hanging them on the hall tree. "When you're here, you're family," Yvonne told Belana. She turned away. "I'm going to see about dinner. Please make yourself at home."

"Come on," Nona said excitedly to Belana, taking her by the hand. "Let's go to my room." Then she looked up at her father. "That is, if Daddy can do without you for a few minutes."

"Sure," said Nick. "I'll go help Mom."

Belana allowed Nona to lead her upstairs, gazing back at Nick, who stood at the bottom of the stairs looking up at her. Her brows rose in a quizzical expression as if to ask him what his daughter was up to. He shrugged his broad shoulders. He apparently had no idea.

Nona's bedroom was large and very neat. She had all the electronics that teens could not live without and her interests were on display, especially in the posters of ballet dancers on her walls. She had dancers from the Dance Theatre of Harlem, Mikhail Baryshnikov, Judith Jamison, Arthur Mitchell, Alvin Ailey and several current dancers from ballet companies around the world. Belana winced when she came to the section devoted entirely to her mother. However, when Nona moved around and could see her expression, she painted on a smile. "I see you really like Mari Tautou," she casually commented.

Nona lit up. "I wish I could see her dance just once before I die," she said fervently.

Belana remembered when that had been her wish, too. But the real Mari Tautou was nothing like the fantasy Mari Tautou. She wasn't, however, going to enlighten a starstruck fifteen-year-old. What if Nona's dreams of one day becoming a prima ballerina were somehow connected with her high opinion of Mari Tautou? She didn't want to be the one to disillusion her. It occurred to her that Nona would find out that Mari Tautou was her mother one day and then Belana would feel obligated to reveal her true relationship with the famous dancer. She would postpone that day as long as possible.

"She is one of the best," Belana allowed. "But don't you think Judith Jamison's career was even more phenomenal? I saw her perform when I was about your age. It was an experience I'll never forget. She was my idol, and still is."

"But Mari is so mysterious," Nona said, smiling wistfully. She went over to her walk-in closet. "I've got to get out of these clothes and put on jeans or something." She glanced back at Belana. "Would you like to change, too? I'm sure I have something that would fit you in here."

Belana doubted that. She was two inches shorter than Nona and definitely fuller in the breasts and the hips. Nona had the type of figure ballet masters loved to see in ballerinas—slim, tall, small waist and with legs that seemed to go on forever. "I'm fine," she told Nona. "I *will* take off these shoes, though."

She sat down on the bed and began removing her three-inch-heeled, spectator-toe pumps. After she'd removed her shoes, she got up and stood in front of her mother's posters, frowning. Mari was so tiny and perfectly formed. When she danced she made it look so effortless, the audience was transported, completely buying into whatever illusion she was selling. Her opinion of her mother *might* be a little biased.

Nona came back into the room fastening the top button on a pair of jeans. She was barefooted and wore a sleeveless Tee in royal blue. "I've looked her up on Google so many times and I still can't find out anything about her personal life except she married a French choreographer named Henri Tautou and that's how she got her last name. And she was born in the United States. It doesn't even say which state. Isn't that unusual?"

Belana wanted to tell her that Mari hid her past because she didn't want her many fans to find out she had left her husband for that French choreographer and abandoned two children. That sort of information would tarnish her precious reputation.

"She's become very popular by being an enigma," Belana said, turning to smile at Nona. "Everybody loves a mystery."

"I saw an online interview of her that was done about five years ago," Nona said, "just before she retired.

It was all in French." She laughed shortly. "That's so cool."

"Look at Mikhail," Belana said, hoping to change the subject. "I swear that man could fly!"

"You didn't do too badly yourself the other night," Nona complimented her.

Belana was warmed by her words. She smiled at Nona. She felt it was time she got down to business. "Your dad tells me you're concerned that if things don't work out between us I'll stop mentoring you."

Nona turned away. "Why'd he have to tell you about that? He's so lame!"

Belana went to her and gently took her by the arm. Nona faced her. "I'm glad he told me," Belana said, "so I can assure you that I'll continue to be your friend no matter what happens. I was your friend before I ever knew you were Nick's daughter, remember?"

Nona's brows knit in a frown. "I'm so embarrassed. That's not something I wanted you to know about me. It makes me sound so childish, and I'm not. I have a real reason to be angry with Dad. I could be living with him, but he keeps making excuses to avoid taking responsibility for me like any dad would. I don't like being a burden on Momma Yvonne all the time. She's still young enough to have a social life, but her social life is cut in half because she always has to consider me before making plans. Dad doesn't think I think about things like that, but I do. I'm sorry, Belana, but the fact that you're dating my dad gives him yet more reasons to not be there for me like he should. You will take up his time, too."

Belana was momentarily speechless. Nona had some good points. As a daughter herself, she was sympathetic. She, too, had felt jealous on occasion when her dad was in the dating pool. She remembered thoroughly despising a couple of the women whom she immediately pegged as gold diggers upon meeting them. When she'd gotten older, though, she realized that her father had a good head on his shoulders and he didn't need her meddling in his affairs.

It was also obvious to Belana that Nick hadn't had time to talk to Nona about moving in with him. She was glad she hadn't inadvertently mentioned it to the girl.

She was going to have to talk with Nick, and soon.

"You're just stuck in the middle of an ongoing battle between my dad and me," Nona continued hotly. "And it wasn't fair of him to bring you into it."

"He just wants you to be happy," Belana said, sounding lame even to her own ears.

"Well, he knows what will make me happy," Nona said. "It's as if my feelings don't matter to him!"

There was a knock on the door.

"Come in!" Nona yelled.

Nick stepped into the room. "I could hear you all the way downstairs, Nona." He closed the door behind him and went to stand in front of his daughter, his arms akimbo. "If you want to yell at someone, yell at me."

Belana was pulling on her shoes. "I think I'll go help Mrs. Reed."

"No," Nona said, grabbing Belana's arm as Belana made her way to the door. "I want you here. If Dad wants to get everything out in the open, you need to be here for that."

Nick nodded toward the door. "Go if you want to," he said, "or you're welcome to stay, your call."

Belana stayed.

Nona let go of her and folded her arms across her chest like her father. Belana noticed how much they looked alike, both as stubborn as mules. "I'll stay only if you let me referee."

"What?" Nona asked, puzzled.

"A fight needs someone to warn the fighters when they're hitting below the belt, or getting out of line in some other way," Belana explained.

This elicited a giggle from Nona. "It sounds weird enough to work. Okay, you can referee."

Belana went to stand between them. "Okay, only one person can speak at a time."

She smiled at Nick. "Ladies first."

When he'd been downstairs helping his mother with dinner by making the salad, Nick had been compelled by her to put on an apron that read Kiss the Cook. He felt silly in it so he took it off and tossed it on to the bed. "All right," he said to Nona. "Let me have it."

"You shouldn't have told Belana how I felt about your relationship. Now she's going to think I'm a selfish brat."

Belana wanted to deny she would ever feel that way about her, but was silent because the referee only interfered when rules were broken.

"Belana would never think that of you," Nick said, to Belana's relief. He sighed and walked up to his daughter and held her by the shoulders. "I am at the end of my rope trying to figure out how to be a better father to you. To my way of thinking, I've done everything I could. My mistake, though, was not taking into consideration what you have been saying for so long, which Belana pointed out to me last night. You need to be living with me, even if I can't be with you 24/7. But when you move in, you're going to have to realize that there will be times I won't be home overnight, or for several nights, for that matter. On those occasions, you will come here and stay with Mom, and not give me any arguments. Am I clear?"

Nona was staring at him with her mouth open in amazement. She closed her mouth and started to say something but instead threw her arms around his neck. "I was all prepared to state my case—I am the captain of the debate team, you know—and then you come out with that and leave my arguments in the dust!"

Nick was laughing and hugging his daughter. He peered at Belana over his daughter's head. She was wiping tears from her wet cheeks.

There was a knock at the door. "I'm coming in," Yvonne announced and followed through with her promise. She stood in the middle of the room, hands on her hips, looking from Nick and Nona, who were still hugging, to Belana, who was still crying.

"Dinner's on the table. Come and get it before I throw it out the back door," she said.

Nick laughed. That's what she used to say when his father was alive. She hadn't used that line in years. His dad—a big, boisterous man who loved to laugh—always got a kick out of it.

"Let's go eat, ladies," he said to Belana and Nona. "We don't want her to throw a perfectly good meal out the door."

They went downstairs.

Chapter 8

"Extension, Belana," Victoria Gables, Belana's dance instructor, said as she walked over to Belana and placed her hand at the small of her back. "Posture, too. What have you been doing on your break? Eating popcorn in front of the TV?"

Belana straightened her back and took a deep breath. Victoria, an African-American woman in her mid-forties, looked like Debbie Allen but had the personality of Attila the Hun, if Attila the Hun were a dance instructor.

Belana was used to Victoria's caustic comments. They had worked together for nearly ten years. Belana paid her well for private instruction, and it was worth every penny because Victoria had trained some of the most accomplished dancers in the business.

"Yeah," Belana replied. "I've been dating this really wonderful man and eating like there's no tomorrow. I admit it."

"Wait, wait, back up," said Victoria. She raised her brows even farther than they already were. She plucked her brows within an inch of their lives, making it appear as if she was in a constant state of surprise. To add to the effect, she wore her long black straightened hair in a ponytail pulled back so severely she could hardly blink. "What man? You're seeing someone?"

Belana lowered her leg, turned with her hand on the barre and raised the opposite leg as high as it would go without pulling a muscle. "It's true, I'm dating a real man with a real job and, believe it or not, a real fifteen-year-old daughter."

"My goodness," said Victoria. "How is that working for you?"

Belana beamed. "What do *you* think?"

"You look like an idiot, so I suppose you're happy," Victoria said sourly. She had nothing against love, but it had been her experience that when a devoted dancer fell in love, especially with a nondancer who didn't understand the life, what came next was a decline in ambition. Victoria believed a dancer without ambition and fierce determination to fight for good roles was just playing at the profession. She didn't waste her time with those kinds of dancers.

"Oh, Vicky, don't be like that. I'm in love, isn't that worth celebrating?"

"Maybe for you, but I'm losing one of my best students."

"No, you're not. I'm not quitting any time soon," said Belana. "Besides that, I may have a new student for you to pummel into shape. The fifteen-year-old daughter shows promise as a dancer."

Victoria narrowed her eyes at Belana. "Don't tease me. Who has she been working with? It's usually too late to do anything with a fifteen-year-old. If they've been taught incorrectly they have to relearn everything. I don't have the patience for that."

Belana grimaced. *That* was an understatement! Smiling again, she said, "She's had competent teachers and, in a way, *you've* been mentoring her for seven months already because I've been teaching her your methods."

"You little thief!" Victoria cried, smiling for the first time. She was secretly delighted Belana had taken to her teachings so well she could in turn teach someone else.

Belana laughed at her reaction. "So, you'll take a look at her and see if I'm right, that she has something special?"

"Bring her with you the next time you come," Victoria said. "Now do your pointe work, and let me see some sweating. You've got to work off those five pounds you've gained. Lord knows what possessed you to eat so much."

"I eat when I'm happy," Belana said.

* * *

"Get in here, why are you so late?" Belana whispered to Erik as she pulled him inside her apartment. "She just phoned and she's on the way up."

"Why are you whispering?" asked Erik, "if she isn't here yet?"

"I don't know!" Belana laughed. Nick was at her side. He and Erik greeted each other and then they all walked farther into the apartment where around thirty of Ana's friends were standing around, looking at Belana for instructions. She had planned this surprise birthday party for Ana, who was turning twenty-five. She scanned the room. No party favors or other decorations in plain view. Now, where to hide thirty people so that they could jump out and yell, "Surprise!" when Ana arrived?

There was no way all those people were going to be able to hide behind her furniture. The space in the living room was too sparsely furnished. She hated claustrophobic rooms with too much furniture and knickknacks in them.

"I'm just going to turn the lights off," she announced.

The doorbell rang. Belana whispered, "Everybody be quiet as mice."

"We can't hear you!" Erik whispered back, messing with her.

"Be quiet!" his sister whispered back as she hurried to the door. Before she turned the lock release, she switched off the lights.

Ana gave her a quizzical look when she stepped inside carrying a large white shopping bag containing art supplies. "Why is it so dark in here?"

That was everyone's cue to yell, "Surprise!" and Belana turned the lights back on.

Ana—tall, lovely, skin the color of toasted almonds, big dark brown eyes, and long, blue-black hair— screamed in fright and then in delight when she saw all of her friends. Belana wasn't sure but she thought her friend said a curse word or two in Italian. Her own Italian wasn't that good. But between Ana's jumping up and down and grabbing Belana to hug her, she felt the surprise had gone over well. Everyone rushed forward to say happy birthday and give the birthday girl warm hugs and kisses which ended up looking like a group hug.

Belana disentangled herself from the human mass of love, grabbed Nick by the hand and led him to the kitchen. She looked back and noticed that Erik was the recipient of a kiss on the cheek from Ana, who was looking at him in a most peculiar fashion.

But Belana didn't have time to analyze that look. She and Nick were going to take the food out to the waiting serving tables in the living room. She'd had the food catered and had hired a bartender, who was at this moment setting up the bar in a corner of the room.

Nick pulled her into his arms once they were alone in the kitchen and kissed her. "I haven't seen you in five days, and we've got to wait until after the party to be alone. I thought I'd at least get one kiss," he said once they parted.

Belana smiled up at him. "I missed you, too." It was October and they had been together a little over two months. She was back at work, rehearsing up to six hours a day, auditioning for roles, going to her private class with Victoria, which was now being shared with Nona. Nick was also busy. He'd been responsible for three major sports stars signing with the agency and the senior partners had offered him a full partnership. He was thinking about it. What he really wanted to do was start his own agency.

More importantly Nona had moved in with him and so far they were not having any problems. When he had to be out of town, she willingly went to stay with her grandmother. No arguments. Nick was content.

They kissed again, losing themselves in each other. Nick's hands were in her thick, wavy hair; hers were caressing his muscular back. He backed her against the marble counter and lifted her so that she was sitting atop it. They continued kissing. Belana wrapped her legs around his waist. Her silk dress was hiked up to her shapely thighs.

Someone cleared his throat.

They broke apart and looked up, embarrassed, and saw Erik standing in the doorway. "No sex in the kitchen," he joked. "I'd never be able to eat in here again."

Nick helped Belana down from the counter. "You're

just in time to help take the food out," Belana told her brother, all business again.

"Yes, ma'am," said Erik, smiling.

Belana gave him her dead-eyes look and he laughed. "Don't," he warned her, "or I'll have to say the dreaded words."

Belana picked up a huge platter of spicy steamed shrimp and handed it to Erik. "Which dreaded words?"

Erik bent down and whispered in her ear, "I told you so."

Belana knew he was referring to the fact that he had been the one who had told her she should give Nick another chance. "So you were right for once in your life!" his sister retorted.

Erik left the kitchen laughing, the tray of shrimp held aloft as though he were a trained waiter. Nick, who had not heard what had transpired between Erik and Belana, picked up a tray of food and followed Belana out to the living room.

The bartender was mixing drinks as fast as he could. The music was blaring, and Ana was talking animatedly with a group of friends, one of whom was Erik. Belana told herself she was not interested in matchmaking. If Ana and Erik got together they would have to do it on their own. But she wished that something positive would happen between the two tonight.

After she and Nick finished piling the two serving tables with food, she grasped him by the hand and said, "Now, I'd like to dance with my man."

A smooth Maxwell groove had just begun. Nick grinned and pulled her close. No one else was dancing, but they didn't care. They moved together as if their bodies had been specially made for each other. Belana had danced with a lot of professional dancers but this was so much better. With Nick she felt free and sensual. The feel of his hand at the small of her back sent lovely prickles of desire coursing through her. His muscular thigh touching hers made her want to get even closer to him.

Nick breathed in the intoxicating scent of her. Her skin, underneath his rough hands, felt like warm silk. In his mind he was already making love to her. This dance was just the prelude.

They were so engrossed in each other that they hadn't noticed the music had stopped a couple minutes ago. They were jolted back to reality when everyone else in the room started clapping, whistling, shouting catcalls and "Get a room!"

"Very funny," Belana groused as she and Nick reluctantly let go of one another. She glared at Erik who was standing suspiciously next to the wall unit that housed the sound system. "Turn the music back on."

Erik hit the switch and Mary J. Blige began serenading them.

For the rest of the night, everyone kept it light, eating and drinking and laughing and simply enjoying each other's company. Belana and Nick shared a love seat in one corner of the room, talking about anything and everything, and from time to time Belana would search the room for Ana and Erik and found them together each time, Ana smiling as though Erik were the most charming man on earth, which Belana seriously doubted what with his asinine behavior tonight. Not that she wouldn't be perfectly happy if Ana became her sister-in-law. But she was not going to get involved.

At around one in the morning, Ana walked up to Belana and hugged her. "You were so sweet to do this for me. I was really missing my family. I think this is the first birthday I've spent without them. But you made it a happy one." She turned around to look at Erik. He was talking to another guy. "I have to go home now, though, because I have a shoot tomorrow and if I don't get eight hours I wake up looking like a raccoon."

Belana wondered if Erik had offered to take Ana home, but swore she wouldn't ask.

She hugged her much taller, five-ten friend and said, "I'm glad you enjoyed yourself. How are you going to get home?"

"Someone offered me a ride," Ana said, once again turning to look at Erik.

"All right, then," Belana said, trying to keep the excitement out of her voice. "I'll call you. Don't forget to take the rest of your cake home with you."

Belana had had the wonderful Lyla Daly of Lyla's Cakes make Ana's birthday cake. It had been the highlight of tonight's menu. A Southern treat: red velvet cake with cream cheese icing. Belana didn't want it in the house for fear she'd finish it off. Homemade cakes were her weakness.

"Oh, no," Ana said, mirroring Belana's thoughts. "That cake is too delicious to come home with me. Send it home with someone who can stand the calories."

Belana laughed and walked her to the door where Erik, having extricated himself from his conversation, was waiting. He kissed Belana's cheek. "Good night, sis, I had a good time."

"Mostly at my expense," Belana said. She playfully shoved him out the door. "And don't come back!" she shouted. Erik and Ana laughed all the way down the hall.

When she turned around, Nick was behind her. He smiled. "Party breaking up?" he asked hopefully. He and Belana, as far as he was concerned, were long overdue for some alone time. Nona was staying with his mother this weekend. Tonight was Friday. He had two nights to spend with the woman he loved and these people were cutting into his time.

"I can't just throw everybody out," Belana whispered.

"Allow me," Nick said. He cleared his throat and said loud enough to be heard over the music, "People, it's time to say good-night!"

Some looked around at him and laughed as if he were joking. They continued dancing and talking animatedly.

Nick was about to try again when Belana grasped him by the arm. "Wait, I've got an idea."

She went over to the bartender who was looking rather haggard after four and a half hours of preparing drinks and handing them over with a smile. His jaw muscles were sore from smiling. So, when Belana walked over and softly asked him to tell a little white lie and say that all the booze was gone, he happily obliged.

He waited until someone else walked up to him to smile and say, "I'm sorry, but the bar is dry."

"What?" asked a guy with curly blond hair. "Are you positive?"

"I'm the one mixing the drinks," said the bartender in menacing tones. He picked up an empty vodka bottle, thereby flexing his huge biceps.

The blond guy held up his hands in defeat. "Okay, you don't have to get testy."

"I do when you're up in my grill telling me I'm a liar," said the bartender.

Belana walked up to them and stood between them as if she had to break up a fight. "I'm sorry, everybody," she called loudly, "but we're out of libations. If you don't mind drinking tap water, please continue partying."

Nick, who was standing beside her, said, "I thought we were trying to get rid of them."

"Wait," Belana said.

Sure enough, the partiers started finishing off the potent potables they had in their hands, setting their glasses down, and heading for the door, or in the case of those who still followed the rules of social decorum, walked up to Belana and thanked her for a lovely evening.

In fifteen minutes, they'd all left.

After the last guest had departed, Belana surveyed the mess they'd left behind: glasses, plates, forks and napkins covered the serving tables, the coffee table and end tables. She went to pick up a discarded plate from the coffee table, and Nick grabbed her wrist. "I'll help you clean up in the morning."

"But look at it," Belana protested. The mess was an affront to her compulsive cleanliness sensibilities.

Nick, not wanting to waste yet more time debating, simply picked her up and began walking to the bedroom. "I'll get roaches," Belana cried, as he carried her away from the mess. "You know New York City cockroaches. They can invade in the middle of the night and rearrange your furniture!"

Nick laughed. "I never liked the couch in that spot, anyway."

Belana laughed and went limp in his arms, back arched and hand thrown dramatically over her forehead. "Okay, I surrender!"

"What a ham," was Nick's opinion of her performance.

In the bedroom he set her down beside the bed and the first thing they did was to get out of their shoes. Then they stood entwined in each other's arms, kissing. Their bodies sang with the need to be as one. Belana used to wonder what true sexual synchronization would feel like because with her other lovers she had not achieved the sheer bliss that she had been told was possible between lovers who were in tune with each other. With Nick, she knew that sublime sensation.

It sounded cheesy, but it was like that old song: she was the magnet and he was steel. She pressed her hands against his hard, muscular chest and moaned with pleasure.

Nick broke off the kiss to caress her cheek and peer down into her beloved face. "Baby, that night we saw each other again, I swore that I would have my say no matter what. You had to know how much I regretted my actions. I don't want to regret anything about my relationship with you, so from now on I'm going to just say what's on my mind. I love you."

Belana gasped. She was unbelievably happy to hear him say that. She opened her mouth to say she loved him, too, but Nick bent his head and kissed her again, interrupting her.

When he raised his head, he smiled at her. "Please don't say you love me if you're not sure. I'm patient, I'll wait."

"I would marry you tomorrow," Belana told him, smiling wonderingly up at him.

Stunned, Nick grinned. "I think I can arrange that," he said softly. Truthfully, he knew judges and politicians who could probably pull it off. However, he'd said that to let her know he was not averse to the notion of marrying her right away.

Belana calmly began unbuttoning his shirt. "We could go to Vegas." She then reached for his belt buckle, but Nick had no patience and quickly got out of his pants himself. He was standing in his boxer briefs and socks now.

"Or fly to Mexico," Nick said, helping her off with the shirt by wriggling his broad shoulders. Belana pulled the shirt off him and tossed it onto the foot of the bed. Now his chest was bare. She bent and kissed him between his pectorals. She felt him quiver at her touch.

"Unzip me," Belana said, turning around to present her back to him. Nick unzipped the pale yellow silk dress and pulled it over her head. Belana took it and gently laid it on the back of the chair sitting in front of her vanity. Nick looked with satisfaction at her golden-brown body in the skimpy lacy bra and bikini panties.

He reached up, tipped her head back, and kissed her throat. Her warm, silky skin smelled faintly of fresh flowers. He breathed her in. Then he flicked his tongue out and licked her. Belana went weak in the knees. An insistent, yet very pleasurable aching began between her legs and she could no longer wait to have him inside of her.

She grasped the waistband of his boxer briefs. Nick smiled, took the hint, and finished undressing himself while Belana slipped out of her bra and panties.

Eyes locked, Belana stepped backward until her legs touched the edge of the bed. She sat down demurely but upon sitting, opened her legs. Nick's gaze lowered. His heartbeat sped up. Formerly she had been the way nature made her, but now she had been shorn except for a patch shaped like a heart. His erection practically stood up and saluted.

Belana smiled and crossed her legs. "You like?"

Nick laughed. "You have to ask?"

Belana looked pointedly at his erection. "I guess not." She got up and retrieved a condom, tore it open, dropped the wrapper on to the nightstand and went to Nick. "Allow me."

She knelt, put the condom at the tip of Nick's manhood, and gently rolled the latex sheath on to him. This done, she kissed his thigh. Nick groaned softly, reached for her hand and helped her to her feet.

He pulled her roughly against him, her breasts crushed against his hard chest. Belana smiled; she liked a lot of physicality during sex. She wanted to sweat and pant and give everything she had to the effort.

Nick threw her on to the bed and straddled her. Their eyes met. He growled and kissed her deeply. Belana, not one to lie down in submission, wrestled him on to his back and straddled him. Rising up, she took his penis in her hand and guided it inside of her. Slowly, she lowered her body on to it until their groins were rubbing together.

"Oh, yeah," she whispered. With her eyes closed, her long, curly hair hanging down her back, and her nipples erect, to Nick she looked like some nameless African goddess in the throes of passion. He tried his best not to come too soon, but it was difficult not to because he was so turned on he was about to burst.

Belana opened her eyes and watched Nick. He was hitting on just the right spot, his thrusts sure and hard, just the way she liked them. How was it that every time they made love it was always as if it were the first time? To her delight, she discovered something new about him with each encounter.

This time she had noticed he liked squeezing her butt as she straddled him. Good thing, because it turned her on as well. The harder he squeezed the closer she came to completion. She felt the intense pressure building. In the beginning it felt far away and she could feel it gaining power with each wonderful thrust. Now it was so close…. She pumped him a bit harder. Nick removed his hands from her bottom and reached up to gently pearl her nipples between his thumbs and forefingers. Then he rose up at the waist and took one of them into his mouth. Belana clutched his head to her breast, it felt good. That's when she came. She let go of his head, Nick lay back flat on his back and met her frantic thrusts with equal passion. Belana collapsed on top of him. He held her, whispering, "I love you. I love you."

He felt the throbbing walls of her vagina. It only made him harder.

Belana breathed against his cheek, "Take what's yours."

Nick easily turned her over on to her back and was inside of her in an instant. Belana sighed with pleasure. How did he do that? His engorged member was right on her sweet spot. She felt inadequately prepared for another meltdown, yet hoped for it.

Nick's body was a well-oiled machine. Powerful muscles playing under glistening dark brown skin, so mesmerizing to watch that Belana almost wished she were a voyeur and not a participant. She wished this only for a second because if she were simply watching she would not be experiencing her second orgasm right…now. Nick let out an impassioned moan and, God's truth, Belana felt the heat of his seed rushing into the tip of the condom. That was a baby, she thought jokingly.

Nick fell on to his side and pulled her into the crook of his arm. They smiled into each other's eyes. "Baby," he said, "just tell me it was a woman who left that bit of artwork on your, um…sweet place."

"What if I said it was a guy?" Belana teased him.

Frowning, he sat up and glared at her. "What!"

"Just kidding, it was a woman," Belana said, laughing and pulling him down for a kiss.

When they came up for air, Nick said, "For future reference, I like you without the grass being mown."

Belana smiled. "It'll grow back."

They spooned. Nick said in her ear, "Tell me about your week. Five days without you is much too long."

"I auditioned for the role of Titania in *A Midsummer Night's Dream*," Belana told him. "I'll find out next week if I got it."

"Do you really want it?" asked Nick.

"So much I can taste it," said Belana with a wistful sigh.

"Then you'll get it," said Nick with confidence.

Chapter 9

The next morning Belana and Nick went for a run together in Central Park. Afterward they came back to her apartment, showered and Nick made breakfast of scrambled eggs and toast. Belana's refrigerator was in sore need of restocking. She had grocery shopping on Saturday's agenda.

While they were eating, her phone rang and she got up to answer it. She picked up the phone on the counter of the kitchen nook and propped her butt on the stool, smiling at Nick as she did so. Not bothering to check Caller ID, she said, "Hello?"

"She says she just wants to be friends," Erik said without preamble. His voice sounded so bereft that Belana, concerned, stood straight up as if poised for action should he tell her he had a gun in his hand and was seriously considering suicide.

"What did you say to her?" she asked softly. She made her voice sound calm even though she wasn't feeling that way.

"I told her how I felt about her," said Erik with a sad sigh. "I feel like a fool for confessing my undying love when all she wants to be is my friend."

"Wait, Erik," Belana cautioned him. "I'm sure she gave you a reason why she just wants to be friends."

"Because she doesn't trust her judgment where men are concerned," Erik provided.

"I was afraid of that," said Belana.

"*Now* you tell me you were afraid of that?" cried Erik. "You couldn't have mentioned it before I made a fool of myself?"

"Well, I thought it might be a possibility given her experience with men. We talked about that, remember? She's been hurt before. Look, sweetie…"

"Uh-oh," said her brother. "You only call me sweetie when you have some really bad news."

"I wouldn't call it bad news," said Belana. "It could eventually be the best thing you could do."

"Go on," said Erik cautiously. "Even though I'm beginning to think I shouldn't take your advice."

"If she wants you to be her friend, then be her friend, Erik. Don't make any romantic overtures. Be there when she needs you."

"How long am I expected to be a dope?" Erik asked.

Belana laughed. "That's not being a dope. You'll at least be a part of her life. Stop thinking that you have to have her now or you won't have her at all. Love takes time."

"But how long, Belana?" Erik insisted on knowing.

"Give her a year," Belana suggested.

"A year?" her brother bellowed.

"What is a year compared to spending the rest of your life with the woman you love?" asked Belana reasonably.

Erik sighed again. "When you put it that way, I guess it's not so long."

"Besides, I'm being pessimistic when I say a year," his sister told him. "I doubt it'll take her that long to realize how wonderful you are."

"Oh, she already knows how wonderful I am," Erik said. "She kissed me and said I deserved someone who didn't have such a poor track record with men. She said she wished I'd told her how I felt before she started dating that pretty-boy actor because she's always been attracted to me."

"See!" cried Belana.

"But what good does that do me when she's sworn off men?" asked Erik helplessly.

"None whatsoever," Belana said, not mincing words. "But there is hope."

"Okay, okay, I'll cling to hope like some drowning sailor hanging on to the last vestiges of his wrecked boat."

"Boat, that's it!" cried Belana, her brain working overtime. "Ana loves boats. And you have that cabin cruiser. Take her on the boat for a weekend cruise, as friends. Don't even look at her with puppy-dog eyes. Just have a good time."

"Do you think she'll go?"

"The girl has a broken heart," Belana said, listing the reasons why. "She's been working like a dog for the past year and is overdue for a real break. She'll go. She likes you and she feels safe with you. Two things a woman values, believe me."

"I'll ask her," Erik decided. "Gotta run, sis, tell Nick hello for me."

"How did you know Nick was here?"

"Please," said Erik, "the way you two were carrying on last night, where else would he be?"

"Erik says hello, Nick," Belana said to Nick.

"Hello, Erik!" Nick called.

Erik laughed on his end. "Bye, baby girl."

"Bye," said Belana and hung up the phone.

She went to sit back down. Her eggs had gotten cold. She got back up to warm them a few seconds in the microwave.

"Nick and Ana are having problems?"

"How did you know about Nick and Ana?"

"They left the party together last night," Nick explained.

"You're very observant." Her eggs warmed, Belana carried her plate back to the kitchen table and sat down.

"I try to be," he said. "I also surf the Net and I know

that Ana just found out her boyfriend cheated on her. That must not be easy for her to deal with, having your personal business all over the Net and the tabloids."

"Yeah, Erik is going to have a hard time breaking through the wall she'll undoubtedly erect around her heart," Belana said with a note of sadness.

Nick reached across the table to grasp her hand. "True love is worth it."

Belana smiled her agreement. She'd just put a forkful of scrambled eggs in her mouth.

The following Tuesday morning when Belana arrived for rehearsals, she was met by one of the company's chief choreographers and told she would be dancing the role of Titania in *A Midsummer Night's Dream*. Belana was so thrilled she practically sailed through that day's full day of rehearsals which lasted six hours with only a break for lunch.

When she got home, she was so tired she could barely drag herself into the shower. But the hot shower revived her somewhat and a bowl of hearty chicken noodle soup chock full of vegetables went a long way toward making her feel like herself again.

She was sitting in front of the TV with it tuned to CNN when she realized she hadn't yet told anyone she had been offered the role of Titania. After she had been given the news she had gone straight to dance class. Over lunch, which she'd shared with Suri and several other dancers, talk had been about the new season and who would be going up for which roles and why wasn't so and so picked over so and so. Sometimes the business could make a dancer very insecure about her abilities. Belana tried to be encouraging to everyone, assuring them that their chance to shine would come someday, too.

Now she sat alone on her couch, not really paying attention to what was on the TV screen, wondering why she was alone on her couch not paying attention to what was on TV. She missed Nick, who was in Seattle. One of his clients, she couldn't remember his name, but he had gone to rehab for alcoholism, was in danger of being let go because he had fallen off the wagon. Nick told her over the phone that he didn't know what he could do, but the client's wife had sounded so distraught, he had had to go.

She could tell by the sound of his voice that he also was upset that one of his clients, and obviously a friend, could lose his livelihood because of alcoholism.

She didn't want to interrupt him.

She picked up the cordless that was on the coffee table. Her father was the person to phone. He and Isobel were at their Connecticut house. Her grandmother, Drusilla, made it her permanent home, but her father and stepmother were only there a few weeks out of the year. They lived mostly in a Manhattan apartment and also loved to stay at their house in Hawaii when they wanted to leave the world behind.

Her stepmother, Isobel, answered the landline number. "Hi, baby, how are you?"

Even the sound of her stepmother's voice soothed

Belana. She'd known her for nearly as long as she'd known her daughter, Elle. Elle had taken both her and Patrice home with her the first Christmas after they'd met and Isobel had welcomed the girls with open arms. She was a fantastic cook and made the girls their favorite dishes and even taught them to cook on weekend visits. They'd made her home in Harlem their getaway from school.

"Hi, Mom," said Belana. "I'm doing really well. How're you and Daddy and Grandma?"

"All well," said Isobel. "Your grandmother's arthritis is acting up but you didn't hear that from me."

She and Belana laughed shortly. Drusilla hated being reminded of her age. She claimed she was as young as she felt and most days she felt like she was thirty, forty on a bad day. She was actually eighty.

"I'm just calling to tell you and Daddy I'll be dancing the role of Titania in *A Midsummer Night's Dream* in December."

Isobel screamed in her ear. She knew Belana had been coveting that role for quite a while. Belana heard her stepmother yelling, "John, John, Belana's going to be Titania!"

Her father, who must have been in his study, Belana guessed, suddenly picked up an extension and cried, "Way to go, Titania! I'm so proud of you."

Belana felt their love. She was reminded of the time her father had told her she was the best Sugar Plum Fairy he'd ever seen. Then she remembered on which occasion that had been and some of her joy dissipated. She wondered if her mother ever thought of her and Erik.

"Thanks, Daddy," she said.

"Listen, Drusilla wants to have Thanksgiving here this year," her father was saying before she realized she'd been daydreaming about her mother. "Invite your gentleman friend."

Belana smiled at her father's terminology. He was old-fashioned in some ways. "Well, I wouldn't want to invite him without his daughter and his mother," she said. "They're like a unit."

Her father's voice was full of cheer. "Bring them all, darling, the more the merrier."

"I'll invite them," Belana promised.

"Wonderful," enthused her father. Then he said, "Is there something else you wanted to tell me? You sound kind of melancholy."

"I was just thinking of Mari," said Belana. "That always makes me sad."

"Darling, you have to let it go," said her father. "She missed out on knowing you and Erik. It's her loss. Don't let it color your enjoyment of your own life." He cleared his throat. "I hear from Erik that you're very fond of your young man."

"I'm in love, Daddy," said Belana, this time with a happy lilt to her voice.

"She's in love, Izzie," said her father, using his nickname for his wife.

"I'm so happy for you," Isobel said on her extension. "We can't wait to meet him."

"Soon," Belana said. She said goodbye shortly after that and picked up the remote and changed the channel from the news to a classic movie on the American Movie Channel. Cary Grant, James Stewart and Katharine Hepburn were having a ball in *The Philadelphia Story*. She was laughing out loud before she knew it.

The day before Thanksgiving, Belana was walking from her morning dance class, about to enter the subway when someone yelled out her name. She turned around and saw Suri running toward her, her dark wavy hair flying behind her. "Belana, are you in a rush to get home? I really needed to talk to someone." Her large brown eyes pleaded with Belana to say she could spare some time. Although Belana wanted to get home to relax a bit, she said yes and they wound up going to The Cupcake Café, a nearby bakery, and ordering cups of coffee.

"What's up?" Belana asked, looking into Suri's eyes.

Unshed tears sat in Suri's lovely eyes. She blinked and soon her cheeks were wet with them. She wiped her face with a paper napkin and forced a smile. "I'm pregnant."

Belana immediately reached across the tiny round table and grasped the other girl's hand. "If there's anything I can do to help, just tell me," she commiserated.

"There's nothing anyone can do," Suri said sadly. She smiled again through her tears. "I don't believe in abortion, so I'm going to have the baby. The father won't be a part of her life, though. He's already told me he's not leaving his wife, and he already has three kids, he doesn't want any more. He accused me of trying to trap him. He said he would make sure his lawyers made my life miserable if I tried to make trouble for him."

"In the form of telling his wife what he's been up to?" Belana guessed.

Suri nodded. "As if I wanted his money!" she cried passionately. "I don't need his stinking money."

"Are you going to be okay raising the baby on your own?" Belana asked, hoping Suri would calm down. Her last outburst had other customers looking nervously their way.

New York City had plenty of nuts but you didn't want to be stuck in a bakery with one of them.

"I'm not going to raise the baby," Suri told her. "I'm putting her up for adoption and then I'm getting on with my career. I'm only twenty-three. I can barely feed myself on what I earn. How could I possibly think of raising a child?"

"But you said you didn't need his stinking money," Belana reminded her.

"I meant that I wouldn't dream of stooping to take his money," Suri explained. "I could actually use financial support."

Belana didn't know what advice she should give Suri, or if she should be giving her advice at all. What if she advised her to go after this guy for financial support and ended up dead? She wouldn't be the first mistress to meet an untimely end when she tried to make trouble for some rich, married guy. Anyway, Suri had said she wasn't keeping the child. Someone with means would adopt a healthy baby. There would probably be hundreds of couples who would want to.

Suri definitely would not be dancing while she was noticeably pregnant, though. She would need funds to live on while she was waiting for her child's birth.

Belana had plenty of money. She'd inherited a twenty-million-dollar trust fund when she had turned twenty-five, and she hadn't even touched the principal. She was living on the interest.

"I'd be happy to help you make ends meet until you can go back to work," Belana told her.

Suri looked shocked. Belana was not surprised. No one she worked with knew she was John Whitaker's daughter. She was another struggling dancer to them.

"I inherited a little money a few years ago," she said to Suri. "It's enough to make my life a bit easier. I don't see why I can't use it to make your life a bit easier, too."

"I don't know, Belana," Suri said reluctantly. "I couldn't say when I could pay you back."

"You don't have to pay me back," Belana told her.

"What? That's insane. You work hard for your money."

"I didn't work for this money, it just sort of fell into my lap," said Belana. She went into her bag and withdrew her checkbook.

Suri began to cry again when she presented her

with a check for fifty thousand dollars. "This is too generous," she said, sniffling.

"You mean you can live on less for a year? In this city?" asked Belana knowingly. She had been to the loft apartment Suri shared with three other girls. Her share of the rent was probably only five hundred a month in the rent-controlled building she lived in. But everything was priced high in the city—food, clothing, transportation. Not to mention doctor's fees. She would have to be under a doctor's care.

"You've got to eat right and keep your doctor's appointments," she said. "You don't want to put your child's health at risk."

Belana could tell Suri hadn't even thought about medical costs.

"You see what I mean?" Suri asked. "I'd never be able to afford to keep this baby."

A wistful quality in the girl's voice made Belana wonder if Suri was being entirely truthful about not wanting to keep her baby, but Belana held her curiosity in check. She would not encourage her by questioning her decision. It wasn't her place to do that.

She rose and placed her hand over Suri's, causing Suri's hand to close over the check. "You're my friend, and I care about you. Take the money, and take care of yourself."

Suri got up and hugged Belana so tightly she could hardly breathe. "I'll pay you back one day," she promised.

"If you want to help someone else someday, fine, but

I've just done what I wanted to with that money. I won't miss it," Belana said with a smile. She extricated herself from their embrace and said, "Hey, are you going home for Thanksgiving?"

Suri was from a small town in upstate New York. She had always dreamed of dancing for a New York City ballet company. "Yeah, I'm going home. I hope my parents take the news well. Five daughters and the baby girl is the one who gets pregnant before marriage. All the rest were married before presenting them with grandchildren. I'll be the shame of the family."

"Don't jump to conclusions," Belana warned. "You might be surprised by their reaction. Single parenthood doesn't have the stigma attached to it that it used to."

Suri took a deep breath and released it. "From your lips to God's ears," she said hopefully.

"Okay," said Belana with a note of finality. "I've got to run." She gave Suri a quick hug. "I know you probably feel ambivalent about this, but congratulations on your good news. I think babies are always a blessing."

Suri smiled, calmer now. "Thank you, Belana."

No amount of reassurances from Belana could make Nick less apprehensive about meeting her father. As he drove, he thought about all the different ways this day could go wrong. No, make that days. Belana had persuaded them to spend the night. Now he had double the time in which to do something embarrassing. Don't forget Nona. She had been behaving herself recently, but she was a wild card. He didn't worry about his mother. His mother was gracious to a fault.

Belana rode up front with him serving as the navigator even though he had a perfectly good navigation system in the SUV. She kept up a line of jovial banter on the two-and-a-half-hour trip, pointing out landmarks, telling anecdotes about when she and Erik were kids and how they always thought going to Connecticut was equal to going on an adventure.

She regaled them about New Haven, Connecticut's finer points, the most well-known being it was the home of Yale University. Her father had gone to Yale. Nick had inwardly cringed upon hearing that. He had gone to a city college on scholarship. There was nothing prestigious about it. He tried to relax, remembering what she'd said about her father being just a man. He was shy, she'd said. Yeah, right. What did John Whitaker have to be shy about?

On the last leg of the trip now, he drove the SUV down a private lane and then they saw the house. No, you couldn't call it a house. Okay, you could call it a house the way they called the White House a house. The Whitaker house was about as big as the White House. The woodwork was white but the bulk of it was made of red brick.

"Wow," cried Nona from the backseat. "Is that a house or a hotel?"

Belana laughed. "It's a house."

"It's gorgeous," said Yvonne, sitting forward. "What do you call that design?"

"It's a mish-mash," said Belana. "When it was first built, I believe they were going for something on the line of Jefferson's home in Virginia, Monticello. When Daddy bought it he made renovations, adding a guest house, a pool and pool house, and did a lot of landscaping that included extensive gardens and even an apple orchard. It was his country retreat. He said he wanted to feel like a gentleman farmer. He doesn't really live here much anymore. But this is my Grandma Drusilla's home. She loves it here."

They parked in front of the house on the circular drive. As soon as Nick shut off the engine, a tall, trim man in jeans, a plaid shirt and a dark jacket followed by a woman about four inches shorter than he was, and wearing black slacks and a black jacket over a bright fuchsia blouse, bounded out of the house followed by two golden retrievers.

Nick looked down at their feet: they were both wearing black hiking boots, the kind that strung up and had thick soles. He figured they did a lot of walking on the property.

"That's Mom and Dad," Belana said, her excitement evident in her voice. "Come on, everybody."

She sprang from the car and in a matter of seconds was being engulfed in her father's arms, then her stepmother's. Nona was right behind her, but Nick paused to give his mother a hand out of the high car. She was petite and complained it was a chore for her to get in and out of.

"This is Nona, Nick's daughter," Nick heard Belana say as he and his mother walked up to them.

"Hello, Nona," said John Whitaker, smiling. He had a kind face. His skin was a medium brown and he had salt-and-pepper hair that he wore natural and cut low to his scalp which showed the wavy texture of it. His eyes, Nick noticed, were dark brown, not whiskey-colored like Belana's. She must have gotten her mother's eyes. In fact, there wasn't much that Belana had physically inherited from her father. When John turned to shake Nick's hand, though, he saw in his eyes what she had gotten from her father. The expression in his eyes was so kind and welcoming that Nick instantly forgot about his earlier fears.

They shook. "It's good to meet you, Mr. Whitaker," he said, smiling.

"Same here, young man," said John, also smiling.

Nick gestured to Yvonne. "This is my mother, Yvonne."

Yvonne stepped forward and shook John's hand, then Isobel's. The three exchanged greetings. She held on to Isobel's hand a moment longer. "What a lovely place you have."

Isobel clasped her hand firmly. "It would be my pleasure to show you around."

The two women strolled off by themselves. Nona ran to catch up with them. John turned to Nick. "It seems my wife is seeing to the ladies. I was thinking of going for a walk before I saw you all pulling up. Won't you join me?"

Nick felt like he needed to stretch his legs after the drive there. "I'd enjoy that," he said, and they began walking in the direction of the stables.

The golden retrievers trailed behind the men.

Belana stood on the circular driveway by herself, having been abandoned by everyone. "What about me?" she pouted. She laughed. She was thrilled everyone had hit it off so well. She went to find her grandmother. Drusilla was probably preparing to hold court in the drawing room. Smaller than the living room, it was her favorite spot in the house. She liked to take tea there every afternoon as though she were a British citizen. She had never set foot in Great Britain.

She found her grandmother in the kitchen, instead, overseeing the preparation of the Thanksgiving feast. With her grandmother in the large space were the family's two live-in staff, Naomi and Penny, both African-American women.

Drusilla, dressed in a tailored pantsuit and comfortable flats, was leaning on her cane stirring something in a Dutch oven atop the stove. "Grandma," Belana said.

Drusilla turned. Her slightly wrinkled café-au-lait-complexioned face broke into a grin. "Well, if it isn't the prodigal daughter," she chided her granddaughter.

"I haven't been away that long," Belana denied, laughing.

She went and bent down to hug her grandmother. Drusilla had a powerful personality, but she was only five-one. And Belana suspected she was shrinking. She looked smaller every time she saw her. "How are you, dearest?" she asked Drusilla.

Drusilla wore thick glasses attached to a chain around her neck. Otherwise, she would be losing them all day long. She put them on now and stared up at Belana. Her eyes appeared larger when she wore them and she reminded Belana vaguely of an owl.

"Passably well," said Drusilla. "The Grim Reaper has my address but he's having trouble finding it."

Belana chuckled. "Well, let's hope he doesn't start using GPS."

"What's that?" asked her grandmother.

"Never mind," said Belana. "What are you doing in here? I'm sure Naomi and Penny can function without you."

Naomi, a tall, hefty woman in her early sixties who had been with Drusilla since she had moved here over twenty years ago, laughed. "I don't think so, Miss Belana. What would we do without her?"

Possibly have fewer headaches, Belana thought with a smile. Her grandmother liked to have a hand in the running of everything on the estate. Belana believed it was her meddlesome nature that was keeping her going.

"How are you, Naomi?"

"Doing well, and how're you?" Naomi countered.

"Just great," said Belana. She looked at the younger woman, Penny, who had been hired only four years ago. "And you, Penny?"

Penny was busy peeling sweet potatoes. She smiled

at Belana. "Excellent," she said. "I heard that you got the role of a lifetime. I'm happy for you."

"Thanks, Penny. Rehearsals are killing me but I have a good feeling about it," Belana told her. In her mid-forties, Penny was an aspiring writer. She knew a little about dreams and how it sometimes took a long time to achieve them. "Still sending out your work?"

Penny nodded. "I'll keep trying until somebody bites."

"You do that. You'll get a book deal one day," Belana said confidently.

"Belana, since you're here, you can make me a pot of tea," Drusilla ordered. "I like the way you brew my Earl Grey."

"I'm on it," Belana said affectionately. "You go into the drawing room and I'll be in there shortly with a tray."

Drusilla took one more look around the kitchen as though she were assessing the state of things, nodded with satisfaction, and turned to leave. "Oh, Naomi, put a few of those lovely cinnamon tea cakes on a plate for me."

"Yes, ma'am," said Naomi, smiling with genuine warmth.

After Drusilla had gone, she and Belana burst out laughing. "She still likes her tea cakes, huh?" said Belana.

"That, and rum in a cup of warm milk just before bed," said Naomi.

Belana busied herself with the tea things while they talked. "How is your family, Naomi?"

Naomi smiled. The thought of her family was obviously a source of joy for her. "Melora, my youngest, just entered Yale. She's pre-med. And my oldest, Gemma, is getting married next June."

"Congratulations," said Belana. Naomi raised her daughters alone after her husband, Peter, a military man, was killed in action. "Gemma recently graduated from college, didn't she?"

"Yes," Naomi confirmed. "She's doing everything so quickly it makes my head spin. She's only twenty-one."

They talked more about family. Then Belana picked up the tea tray and went to join Drusilla in the drawing room.

"This is Pegasus," said John, fondly rubbing the nose of a white stallion with a flowing mane. The handsome beast whinnied and seemed to press its nose affectionately into John's palm.

The stables housed six horses and it was evident that John Whitaker spared no expense on the horses' accommodations. It had central heat and air, and the spacious stalls were obviously cleaned frequently. The smell of horse manure was faint but nowhere near as offensive as it would be in a less-maintained stable. The overpowering odor here was of hay.

"They're all beautiful animals," said Nick.

"I'm afraid I don't get to ride them often enough,"

said John. "I've been forced to hire college students to exercise them daily."

"You're a busy man."

"Yes, but busy men have to take the time to enjoy the fruits of their labors. I've gotten much better at that since I married Isobel, but I still have a long way to go. I was so used to being a workaholic. It was the air I breathed. I didn't think my life was normal unless I was constantly working. I hope you know when to quit."

"I have to admit, I'm not there yet, either," Nick told him. "I work too much, and I know it. I was recently offered a partnership in my firm and I haven't accepted it yet because I know it means they'll only work me harder."

John laughed shortly. "You've got it. That would be their license to work you like a dog. I hear you're a sports agent. Who are some of the athletes you work with?"

Nick noticed that the golden retrievers had found a spot in the corner of the stable and lain down. The mood was tranquil. Nick thought that odd. Didn't horses get nervous around dogs? But the animals were comfortable in each other's presence.

He had lost his nervousness, too. Maybe it was being in John Whitaker's company that had a calming effect on those around him, animal and human alike. For certain, he was the most centered man he'd ever met. Did that kind of self-assurance come with age or with great wealth?

Nick named some of his clients. John nodded,

recognizing the names. "I heard about Calvin Pruitt's troubles. I hope he can find a way to save himself. He seems like a good man."

"He is," said Nick. "I'm still praying for him."

Chapter 10

Erik and Ana arrived at around four in the afternoon to find Drusilla and Belana enjoying a cup of tea and conversation in the drawing room. Belana told them everyone else was on the grounds somewhere; where, she didn't know.

After introducing his grandmother to Ana, whom she'd never met before, and a quick visit with his sister and grandmother, Erik left Ana with them and went to locate his father who he guessed was with the horses. His father always worried about them in cold weather even though they were housed in a climate-controlled facility.

Ana, looking fresh in skinny blue jeans, a short-sleeve cashmere sweater in a deep shade of purple and black designer boots, sat down and Belana poured her a cup of tea.

"How was your trip?" Belana asked.

Ana smiled and said, "Erik kept me laughing all the way here." Although her English was very good, Ana still had a faint Italian accent and it got thicker when she was upset. She was upset, and Belana's curiosity was piqued. What could have happened on the drive here to upset her? Had Erik broached the subject of pursuing a romantic relationship with her again? No, Erik wasn't that insensitive. Then what was wrong?

By this time, Drusilla had fallen asleep in her comfortable overstuffed chair. She often took catnaps during the day. When she awakened, she would swear she had not been sleeping, only resting her eyes.

"What's the matter?" Belana asked Ana.

Ana looked her in the eyes. "Jack," she said as a little moan escaped. "I read on AOL this morning that he married the girl he left me for."

Belana cursed her aversion to the internet. If she checked her emails more often she would have seen the article and been prepared for this.

"That bastard," she said under her breath.

"Yes," Ana said, "he is. He told *me* he wasn't ready for that kind of commitment. Well, maybe not with me, but he was ready for one with her?" She wiped the corners of her eyes with one of the cloth napkins from the tea tray. Looking appealingly at Belana, she asked, "What has she got that I haven't?"

The age-old question, Belana thought. Women have

been wondering that for as long as men have been throwing them over for another woman. The fault, Belana believed, didn't lie with the women but the men. They had played with that toy long enough. They had gotten bored and wanted another one to play with. "In the state of mind you're in right now, you might not believe this," Belana said, "but there's nothing at all wrong with you, Ana. Jack's the one. He's an asshole. Unfortunately, some men are born assholes. I used to think it was a tendency that they could grow out of, the assholes, I mean, but they never outgrow it. Now, one day you will fall in love with a man who isn't one and you'll learn the difference. That man would never hurt you. He'll cherish you. And thank God he found you."

"Amen to that!" Drusilla said, sitting up in her chair. She yawned. "Was I sleeping?"

"No," said Belana, straight-faced. "You were just resting your eyes."

Drusilla laughed. "Jack Russo wasn't good enough for you," she told Ana.

"Grandma, you follow the tabloids?" asked Belana incredulously.

"He's moderately good-looking," was Drusilla's considered opinion. At eighty she had seen a lot of men come and go. "But his fame relies on his physical appearance. He can't act his way out of a paper bag." She reached for Ana's hand and Ana gave it to her. "You, my dear girl, are not a flash in the pan. His light is going out while yours will shine brightly for many years to come. So, I don't want to see you moping over such a fool."

Ana sat up straighter and smiled, feeling better. "You're right, Mrs. Whitaker, I need to quit being such a crybaby. He doesn't deserve my tears."

"The best revenge, and who doesn't love a little revenge, is living well," Drusilla told her. "That's not just an old adage, it's true. Live your life to the fullest, child, and you'll be ready for love when it comes along."

Ana was nodding as though she were seated at the feet of a guru and benefiting from her wisdom. Belana smiled to herself: her grandmother, the sage.

Ana cleared her throat. "Umm, Mrs. Whitaker, I know we've just met but I would love to sketch you. I'm an amateur artist and I love drawing people with interesting faces. It won't take long, I promise."

"Amateur?" Belana cried. "Grandma, she should be showing at the best galleries in New York City!"

"Oh, I don't know about that," said Ana modestly.

Belana almost laughed when her grandmother preened and said in as nonchalant a tone as she could muster, "If you really want to, dear. I've got nothing but time."

Ana immediately went into her voluminous bag and retrieved a large sketch pad and charcoal pencils. She smiled warmly at Drusilla. "Thank you," she said gratefully.

Dinner was held in the formal dining room. Dressing up wasn't required and the atmosphere was relaxed.

John carved the turkey and the ham, and the rest of the dishes were brought to the table by Naomi and Penny, after which the diners served themselves.

John sat at one end of the long table and his mother at the other. Next to John was Isobel. Drusilla, who'd taken a liking to Nick upon meeting him, had asked him to sit next to her. Belana made sure she was sitting on Nick's other side to keep an ear open for Drusilla's tendency to ask too many personal questions. Drusilla felt that with age came privilege and the greatest privilege of all was saying exactly what was on her mind without editing it. On opposite sides of the table sat Ana and Erik and Yvonne and Nona.

"You must get your height from your father," Drusilla said to Nick soon after the blessing had been said.

"There are tall people on both sides of the family," Nick said. He smiled in his mother's direction. "Mom says she drew the short straw."

"I know how she feels," said Drusilla. "I always wanted to be around five-eight or nine, but I stopped growing at five-two and I think I've shrunk over the years."

I knew it! Belana thought.

"I would have been taller but I had rickets when I was a child and that stunted my growth," Drusilla continued. "Have you ever heard of rickets?"

"It's a bone disease, isn't it?" Nick asked.

"Yes, caused by calcium deficiency and Vitamin D deficiency," Drusilla confirmed. "I was lucky, they caught it in time and I wasn't left with deformed bones, but my growth was severely stunted. All of my brothers and sisters were much taller. So, ironically, John gets his height from my side of the family. His own father was only five-eight, but that was tall enough for me."

Nick had gotten comfortable with Drusilla. He found her to be very sweet and charming. He even thought she might be flirting with him, unless she had something in her eye. She'd winked at him several times since they'd met.

"So," said Drusilla, "I can see from looking at your lovely daughter that you're capable of fathering beautiful children. Do you look forward to having more? Perhaps two or three?"

"Grandma," exclaimed Belana. "You've just met Nick. Do you think that's an appropriate question to ask?"

Belana looked at Nick. He was smiling as if her grandmother's question hadn't embarrassed him in the least. In fact, he appeared as though he was having a hard time containing his laughter.

"I'm sorry," Drusilla said to Nick, smiling. "It's just that I'm eighty years old and an old person needs something to look forward to. It's what gets us out of bed each morning, the prospect of something new happening in our lives."

"I understand," Nick assured her, taking her small hand in his. "And the answer is yes, I would like more children someday, with the right woman."

Drusilla smiled in Belana's direction. Belana blushed. She was glad Nick was being so patient with her outspoken grandmother. However, she knew what her grandmother would say to her once she had her alone. "I don't have time to be pussyfooting around with you and Erik dragging your feet when it comes to giving me a great-grandchild. You're both way overdue. Marry that boy and give me a great-grandchild!" She was getting feisty in her old age.

"That's nice to know," Drusilla said to Nick in her sweetest tones. "Now, I'll let you eat your dinner and quit asking nosy questions. My granddaughter's shooting daggers at me with her eyes."

"Behave!" Belana gently admonished her grandmother.

Drusilla laughed and picked up her knife and fork to cut off a sliver of Virginia ham and put it in her mouth. "Mmm, that's delicious."

Belana mirrored her grandmother's actions and tasted the ham, too. "Yes, it's very tasty."

Drusilla put down her utensils and said, "I hate polite conversation." She looked at Nick pointedly. "This right woman that you mentioned, could she be my granddaughter, perhaps?"

Nick did laugh this time. "The one and the only," he said.

"Good," said Drusilla, "because you would make beautiful children together."

Nona, on the other end of the table, heard the word "children," and her ears perked up. What were they saying about children? Was Belana going to have a baby? Her heart started beating rapidly. She was nearly

sixteen. She definitely didn't want to be the sister of a…
baby! It would be beyond embarrassing explaining that
the baby in the stroller at the park was her little sister
or little brother. Couldn't adults date without making
other kids? It was ridiculous. Then she caught herself
before she blew a fuse. She could be panicking for no
reason. Just because they were talking about children
didn't mean Belana was pregnant. Of course Belana
wasn't pregnant! She was getting ready to dance the
role of a lifetime. No self-respecting ballerina would
give up the chance to be Titania! She most definitely
wouldn't if she were in Belana's place.

Yvonne, seeing the look of consternation on her
granddaughter's face, asked, "Is something the matter?"

"No," Nona said quickly. "This food is so good, I'm
just eating too fast, I think."

"Then slow down," said Momma Yvonne, "or you'll
get indigestion."

Back at Belana's end of the table, Nick was saying,
"I love your granddaughter, Mrs. Whitaker, and I'm
sure that when we decide to take our relationship to
another level, you will be among the first we share the
news with."

Drusilla smiled at Belana. "He said he loves you."

"I heard him."

"Do you love him, too?"

Belana smiled at Nick. "Yes, I love him with all my
heart."

To her utter astonishment, her grandmother started

crying. Belana was so stunned she shot up, nearly toppling her chair, which she had to right before it crashed to the floor. "Grandma, are you all right?"

Drusilla waved her granddaughter back down. "I'm okay. It's just that I never thought I'd hear you say those words." She smiled at Nick. "You must be very special, Nicolas Reed."

Nick was touched. He gently clasped her hand in his again. "Not special," he said. "But very lucky."

"You have my permission to marry my grand-daughter," Drusilla said. "Not right away, of course. But whenever you two decide the time is right. I'm giving my blessings now because the Grim Reaper has my address. He's just having a hard time finding it. He could get smarter any day now."

"Stop trying to manipulate us by throwing out the death card," Belana said, laughing. "Really, Grandma, you should be ashamed of yourself."

"At my age," said Drusilla, "it's not easy to be shamed. I've seen just about everything and nothing surprises me anymore. I know what's important and what isn't. Nobody's going to say I wish I had procrastinated a little longer when they're knocking at St. Peter's gate. They're going to say, I wish I had gone ahead and done this or done that! What a coward I was, not taking more risks."

Belana didn't comment on that because her grand-mother was right. She had nearly lost Nick forever because she had been a coward and been unwilling to risk her feelings and confess that she had been wrong. They had wasted eight months because of her cowardice.

She squeezed her grandmother's hand. "You're right."

"I know I'm right," said Drusilla. "Now, eat."

After dinner, the men went into the library where they gathered around the big-screen TV to watch football, a Thanksgiving tradition, and the women went downstairs to the home theater to put on a film. Belana and Nona went through the DVD collection and wound up choosing *For the Love of Ivy* starring Sidney Poitier and Abby Lincoln. "I've never seen anything with Abby Lincoln in it," said Nona. She was into classic movies, though, and enjoyed discovering a new one. Her grandmother had weaned her on the classics like *To Kill a Mockingbird, Imitation of Life,* and *In the Heat of the Night.*

By the middle of the film, Drusilla announced it was past her bedtime and asked Belana to accompany her upstairs.

They met Erik on the stairs. "Erik," Drusilla said in her commanding way, "I like Ana Corelli. I think you like her, too. *Do* something about it."

Erik looked accusingly at Belana. "Did you tell her?"

"No," Belana cried. "I swear I haven't mentioned a thing to this witchy woman."

Drusilla laughed. "You children are so naive. Nothing escapes me. When I stop noticing things like that it'll be time to put me away."

"We're never going to put you away," Belana assured her as they continued upstairs. Erik turned around, deciding to help Belana tuck their grandmother in.

"Never," he agreed. "Nobody would take you."

This made Drusilla laugh harder.

Later that night after everyone had gone to bed, Belana sneaked across the hall to Nick's room and tapped lightly on the door. He cracked it, and she slipped inside.

At once, they were in one another's arms, kissing hungrily. Nick wore pajamas. It was a cold night. But he usually slept only in pajama bottoms or nothing at all. Belana was in a short, white silken nightgown with spaghetti straps. It shimmered in the dim lighting of the bedroom. "You've got to go," Nick said, surprising Belana. She could tell by the bulge in his pajama bottoms that he really wanted her to stay.

She kissed him again, this time ending with his lower lip between her teeth. That usually drove him crazy. He'd end up kissing her breath away. This time, however, he set her away from him. "I'm serious," he said. "I can't do it in your father's house."

Belana smiled and let go of him. "I understand. I've never done it with my family under the same roof, either. Then again, I've never brought the man I love home."

She watched his face. She knew he was at war with his conscience. She turned and walked back to the door. "All right, good night."

"Belana, I love you," Nick said, going to her and

taking her by the shoulders. "But I don't think it would go over well with your family if they found I'd made love to you while we were here."

"They know we're making love, Nick."

"Yeah, but what kind of man would I be if I couldn't control my libido for an overnight stay in your father's house? This is important to me."

"Can I get another kiss?"

He kissed her on the forehead and let go of her. Belana backed away. "By the way, I apologize for my grandmother. She takes a little getting used to."

Nick smiled. "She's wonderful. She was only saying what was on everybody's mind, anyway. I like her honesty."

"And she was flirting with you all night," Belana said with a laugh.

"Then she *was* winking at me!" Nick said. "I wondered if something was wrong with her eye or she was actually winking at me."

"Oh, she's a big flirt. She loves handsome men." She walked up and quickly kissed him on that dimple in his chin. "I'm going now."

Nick smiled ruefully. "Tomorrow night?"

"Is Nona staying with your mother for the weekend?"

"Yes."

"Okay, then tomorrow night. I have a problem doing it with her in the house. Here? We're way down at the other end of the house. She wouldn't hear us. There, she's right next door."

"The logistics of this relationship could get hairy," Nick agreed.

"We can't get into that right now," Belana told him. "I want you too much. I've got to go." With that, she left, closing the door firmly behind her.

Nick reached for the doorknob, but allowed his hand to fall to his side. It was best to practice abstinence while here. He turned and walked over to the bed where he climbed in and switched off the nightstand light. Sighing when his head hit the pillow, he wondered if Belana would leave her door unlocked for him tonight should he change his mind.

Belana returned to her bedroom and closed the door, leaving it unlocked. She got into bed and picked up her cell phone which had been charging on the nightstand. Going through the messages, she saw one from Patrice and listened closely.

"Hey, girl, hope you're having a great Thanksgiving in Connecticut. Isn't it supposed to be Christmas in Connecticut? T.K. and I are in Albuquerque. His family came with us this time. We'll spend Christmas at his parents' house in L.A. Yes, we will fly out to see your debut as Titania in early December. By that time I might be looking a bit rounder. Bye now, love you much!"

Belana screamed with delight and her fingers flew over the keys, punching in Patrice's cell phone number.

Patrice answered on the second ring. "Howdy!"

"Howdy?" Belana cried. "Two minutes in New Mexico and you revert to your cowboy slang?" she screamed in Patrice's ear. "You're pregnant. That means you were probably pregnant when we were on Mykonos."

"I was," Patrice confirmed, sounding very happy about it. "There I was, talking about my five-year plan, and I already had a bun in the oven. T.K. is on cloud nine. Seriously, I've never seen him grin so much."

"It's wonderful news," Belana said. "I couldn't be happier for you." Her tone more serious, she asked, "How are you feeling about it?"

"I'm in a place of peace," said Patrice. Belana could hear the smile in her voice. "I was shocked, of course, because I thought we were doing everything to prevent a pregnancy. We obviously slipped up."

"It's what Elle was talking about," Belana said. "Remember? She said most pregnancies weren't planned. You're a statistic now, girlfriend."

Patrice laughed. "A happy statistic, that's me."

"I hereby volunteer for babysitting duties whenever you need a break and our schedules allow," Belana offered.

"That's good to know," Patrice said warmly. "You *will* be a joint godmother with Elle?"

"Just like she asked us to be for Ari," Belana recalled.

"Yes," Patrice said, "that way if something should happen to me and T.K., she'll be doubly taken care of."

"Nothing's going to happen to you and T.K.," Belana said, "but yes, I would be proud to be her godmother.

We're referring to the baby as a girl. Do you already know the sex?"

"No, I can't explain it, but I simply feel that it's going to be a girl," Patrice told her.

"We'll see in… How many months?"

"I'm four months along according to my doctor," Patrice supplied.

Belana counted the months in her head. "Then you're going to have an April or a May baby."

"The projected date is April 28th, but I was told the first baby is sometimes late."

"Before you're done, you're going to be talking like Elle who was a repository of all things 'baby' when she was carrying Ari."

"I know," said Patrice. "I'm already making myself sick with my obsession with baby books. I must have every one that's ever been published—You and Your Baby; What to Expect When You're Expecting…name it and I have it. But T.K. is even weirder than I am. He's convinced it's a boy. He's already bought season tickets to the Lakers for him."

"Oh, that's just pitiful," said Belana, laughing.

"Isn't it?"

"Did I hear my name?" T.K.'s voice suddenly said. "Hello, Belana. Still dating Nick?"

"Yes, I am," Belana said, feigning indignation. "Why wouldn't I be?"

"Because you usually would have kicked a guy to the curb by now," T.K. told her, chuckling.

Belana wasn't offended by her friend's husband's

candor. He was right, her modus operandi used to be to have gotten rid of a guy by now. "I think I'll keep this one," she told him.

"Good for you!" said T.K. good-naturedly. "You know we love you, right?"

"I love you guys, too. I know you're going to be great parents." In a way, they had already proven to be great parents because T.K. and Patrice often took care of T.K.'s brother's child. His brother had been killed a few years ago. But at the time of his death, his girlfriend had been carrying his child. T.K. took responsibility for his brother's child and offered to support the girlfriend and the child. He and Patrice were helping to support them to this day.

T.K. put Patrice back on the line and she and Belana talked a bit longer about her impending motherhood, then Belana said good-night.

She lay in bed, staring up at the ceiling, smiling. One day, that could be her.

Chapter 11

December proved to be the busiest month of the year for both Belana and Nick. The first week of December found Belana being fitted for costumes, going through dress rehearsals, enduring day-long dance classes, while trying to find the time to be with Nick. Her schedule was so jam-packed that she barely had time to eat, but she still had to eat healthily and get sufficient calories because it was what she put in her body that fueled her strength to dance. She couldn't afford to become sluggish now.

At the end of the first week in December, Nick had to fly to Los Angeles to put the finishing touches on a deal for one of his long-time clients who was being traded to another team. He'd left on Thursday and was to return on Saturday. However, as Belana was leaving a late rehearsal on Friday afternoon, her cell phone rang and it was Nick telling her he was going to be home that night instead of tomorrow. Belana was glad to hear it and instead of a quiet night home alone, she decided to surprise Nick when he got home with a meal cooked by her own hands. By that time in their relationship, they had exchanged keys so she didn't worry about being able to get into his apartment. She had to time it just right, though. He said he would be home at around seven that evening. It was four now. She had to go home, get a change of clothing and then do the shopping for the items needed for the meal before heading over to Nick's apartment. Luckily, they both lived on the Upper West Side. She hired a taxi and had the driver wait at every stop while she ran around like a crazy person.

Finally, at five-thirty, she was on the way to Nick's place. She sat back on the seat in the cab and breathed a sigh of relief. A night alone with Nick was just what she needed to get her mind right for next week's debut. She was wound tightly. The ballet critic for a major NYC paper was saying that if she managed to be magical in her role as Titania then *A Midsummer Night's Dream* would be the hit of the season. It made Belana nervous when a critic singled her out like that when the success of a ballet depended on the entire company, not just the principal dancers. She understood why the critic had written the article in that manner, though, to garner publicity for her column. Everybody was looking for their big break.

They arrived at Nick's building and Belana climbed out of the cab, pulling the packages and her overnight bag with her. She double-checked to make sure she hadn't left anything on the cab's seat, then closed the door and paid the driver.

"Thank you!"

A few minutes later she was standing at the door of Nick's apartment. *Wait a minute,* she thought. She could have sworn she heard music being played inside. Maybe Nick had left the radio on. Some people left the radio on to fool thieves into believing the house was occupied instead of empty and ripe for the picking.

She shrugged it off and put the key in the keyhole. She had set the heavier grocery bag on the floor while she opened the door. She propped the door open and bent and picked up the heavy bag then gathered the rest of her packages in her arms.

She walked into the foyer and set the bags on the foyer table. She heard a crash in the direction of the living room, like the sound of glass hitting the hardwood floor.

Fear prickled her spine. There could be someone in here. She searched frantically for something to protect herself with. She had a small container of pepper spray in her shoulder bag. She quickly found it and twisted the cap off, and began to slowly advance farther into the apartment, her finger poised over the trigger, ready to spray whoever jumped out at her. The pale evening light that lit the apartment spilled on to the floor, casting weird shadows. On the floor next to the sofa was a broken lamp. That must have been the sound of breaking glass that she'd earlier heard.

Suddenly, a young black man stepped into her line of sight, holding his hands up to show her he didn't have a weapon, no doubt. He was tall and muscular and more disturbing than his size was the fact that he was barechested and barefooted. All he had on was a pair of jeans.

"What the hell are you doing here?" Belana yelled. She walked forward, he moved backward. "Speak up," she shouted, "or I'm going to spray you." She had never had a reason to use the pepper spray. She had been carrying it around for three years or more. The darn thing might malfunction when she hit the nozzle and spray her instead of the guy. He didn't say a word, just kept looking behind him. Belana worried that he might not be alone. He could have an accomplice waiting to jump out and grab her while she was distracted by the half-naked guy.

She put her finger on the trigger anyway and pointed it at him. "I'm gonna count to three: one, two... three!"

She pressed the trigger and a stream of liquid shot into the guy's face. He screamed and began rubbing at his eyes and doing a drunken dance around the room that had him blindly crashing into furniture and howling anew when he stubbed his toe.

Belana continued to spray. Was there such a thing as too much pepper spray when someone was threatening your life?

"Belana, stop!" yelled a feminine voice.

Belana jerked to the right. Running from the direction of the hallway was Nona.

She lowered the almost empty pepper spray canister. "Nona, what are you doing here? Don't get close to that guy. What are you doing?"

Nona was kneeling next to the guy and speaking consolingly to him.

Belana got the picture then. Nona, who also had a key to her father's apartment, had taken advantage of her father being out of town to bring her boy here for an afternoon tryst. Belana didn't like to think about a sixteen-year-old girl involved in a tryst, but she wasn't blind.

Nona glared up at her. "He's my boyfriend, okay? We just wanted to go someplace where we could be alone."

Belana put down the canister and hurried into the kitchen to wet a towel. She returned and handed the towel to Nona. "Here, hold this over his eyes. I'll call a cab and we'll take him to the emergency room. I hear they can neutralize the chemicals in pepper spray."

Nona snatched the towel from her grasp. "You're crazy, you know that? What are you doing here? Left something here the last time you spent the night?"

She and Nick had never spent the night here. But that wasn't any of Nona's business. "Don't try to make this about me," Belana told her, not caring that the girl was fixing her with a hateful glare. "You're only sixteen. You shouldn't be bringing guys back to your house.

Do you know how dangerous that could be? Girls have been killed when they trusted the wrong guy!"

"I told you, he's my boyfriend!"

"I didn't know you had a boyfriend."

"You don't know everything about me, just like I don't know everything about you!"

"Has your dad met this guy?"

Nona cut her eyes at her. Belana knew then that Nick hadn't met him and from the looks of things Nona had not planned on introducing them anytime soon.

"How old is he?"

"Can you get me to the emergency room before you start discussing my vital statistics?" asked the guy who sounded like he was in a lot of pain.

Stuff works, thought Belana facetiously. If he had spoken up she wouldn't have sprayed him. "Look, I'm sorry, but until you tell me how old you are, we aren't going anywhere."

"Belana, you're not my mother and you can't hold us prisoner. We're going," said Nona, yanking on the guy's arm. He staggered to his feet and Nona began guiding him to the door.

"Okay," said Belana, blocking their way, "I can't make you stay but your father is going to be here in about an hour and I'm not letting you out of my sight until he gets here."

Nona's eyes stretched in panic. "Oh, my God, Vincent, I'm so sorry I talked you into this. My dad is going to kill us!"

"You talked *him* into it?" Belana said, incredulous.

"All the girls I hang with have experience," Nona cried in her defense. "I'm the only one who doesn't. I just wanted to do it and get it over with."

"Just so you'd fit in?" Belana asked. "I thought you were smarter than that."

"I am smart," said Nona. "I picked a guy who also has no experience and we were going to use condoms."

"Nona, if you're gonna tell everybody I'm a geek, I wish you'd do it in a cab on the way to the hospital," said Vincent.

Belana breathed a sigh of relief. Nona had said "going to," which could mean they hadn't done anything yet. She had caught them before they'd done the deed.

"He's right, let's go," Belana conceded. "But I'm calling your dad and telling him where to meet us."

"All right," Nona said. "I can't let Vincent suffer. But I hate you for this, Belana. I'll never forgive you for breaking in here like a crazed superhero and spoiling everything."

"I'll just have to tolerate your hating me," Belana told her. "Because I love you and I'm not going stand aside while you make the biggest mistake of your life. Now help him get dressed so we can get out of here."

A short while later, Vincent was dressed and Belana pulled the door closed after them and made sure it was locked.

They were in the hallway now moving swiftly with Vincent between them toward the elevator. "I can't understand you," Belana said. "If you were curious about sex why didn't you talk to your dad or your grandmother? Either one would have listened and tried to offer suggestions on how to survive high school without compromising your virtue."

"A girl's virtue is not worth much these days," Nona told her. "Not when you're ridiculed every day because you're different."

"I hate this," Belana complained passionately as she pressed the down button on the panel in the elevator. She was glad they were alone because what she had to say was for Nona's and Vincent's ears only. "This is a screwed-up society if being a virgin is now considered a bad thing to be. Have you ever thought that misery loves company? They're trying to make you like them because they will feel so much better about themselves when everybody's in the same boat. Dare to be different! You don't have to kowtow under peer pressure."

"It's my choice," Nona insisted. "And Vincent was ready, too. Look at him. He's a hottie, but a hottie with no experience. Do you know how humiliating it is for him to deal with guys in the locker room? They call him queer because he's still a virgin. It's hell."

"It's hell," Vincent agreed. "Hey, I didn't know you thought I was a hottie."

"That's beside the point," Nona said. She looked at Belana. "How can you judge us? You and Daddy aren't platonic friends."

"No, and we're not sixteen, either. We're way past the age of consent. But I'm not going to discuss our relationship right now. We're talking about you. Your dad is trying his best to be a good father, and you go behind his back and take a guy to your home when he's out of town. How do you think he's going to react to that?"

"He's going to be furious," said Nona. "He would be furious anyway when he found out I was sexually active."

"But you're not."

"What?"

"Sexually active."

"No, you ruined that, remember?"

"Just checking."

Nona smiled in spite of herself. "You know, you can be very annoying when you want to be."

"Thank you," Belana said as though her insult were a compliment.

The elevator doors slid open and they were about to step off the conveyance when Nick strode through the entrance.

"I thought you said an hour," Nona said, glaring at Belana.

"He was quicker than I thought he would be," Belana said, and then she steeled herself for the coming conflagration.

Nick was weary from his trip. All he wanted was a hot bath, a hot meal, and Belana lying next to him in bed. He was looking down and didn't see what was unfolding before him at first. Then he heard a gasp and wondered why the sound was vaguely familiar to him. He looked up and saw his daughter holding on to a big, muscular guy holding a towel over his eyes, and Belana on the other side, looking like a deer caught in headlights. His heart seemed to plummet to the pit of his stomach. He knew instinctively that something was terribly wrong.

They stepped off the elevator, both of them smiling like fools, fools caught red-handed. He couldn't see whether the guy was chagrined at his appearance as well because his face was obscured by the towel. Nick controlled the anger that was bubbling up. He stood in front of them, one hand gripping his overnight bag, the other balled into a fist.

"What do we have here?" he asked calmly.

Belana and Nona tried to talk simultaneously, which came out sounding like someone spinning a record backwards. Irritated by their performance, the muscles worked in his strong jaw. "One at a time," he instructed.

"Belana sprayed Vincent in the eyes with pepper spray when she mistakenly took him for a thief," Nona said hurriedly.

Nick let that sink in. Then he turned to Belana. "I didn't know you would be here," he said. He didn't know his daughter would be here, either, but he would get to that later.

"I was going to surprise you with a meal," Belana said. She started to say more, but he held up his hand, stopping her. What she had said made sense to him. He had phoned and told her he would be coming home early. It would have been a nice surprise to find her in his place when he'd gotten there. Nona on the other hand had not known he was coming home early. She was supposed to be in Harlem at his mother's house, or out with her friends on a Friday evening. She wasn't supposed to be on the Upper West Side.

Nick set his bag down and regarded his daughter. "You didn't know I was coming home. How did you happen to be here the same time as Belana? Did she phone you and tell you I was coming home early?"

"No, Daddy," said Nona, attempting a weak smile.

"Then it stands to reason that Belana didn't know you were here."

"No, she didn't, Daddy."

"Who's the guy?"

"He's a friend from school, Vincent Hoynes."

"What is Vincent doing with you?"

"We're dating," Nona said, looking down.

"You can't date yet. You can only go on group dates," Nick stated.

"I know," Nona said. "I broke the rules, I'm sorry."

"How far did you go in breaking the rules?" Nick wanted to know. "Why did Belana feel it necessary to spray a teen boy in the eyes with pepper spray? Why is his shirt on crooked? And his shoes untied?" he shouted.

Belana trembled, let alone Nona. She tried to appeal to his humanity. "Nick, Vincent's in pain. I don't know how bad that stuff is, it could lead to a permanent injury and I don't want that on my conscience. Let's get him to the hospital and we can continue your line of questioning later, please?" she pleaded.

Nick relented. "Get my bag, Nona," he ordered his daughter as he took charge of Vincent who, though nearly as tall as he was, flinched when he grabbed him.

Two hours later, Belana, Nick and Nona were still waiting for Vincent to return. A nurse had taken him away, assuring them that they indeed could help him. They apparently saw a lot of patients like him.

"Yeah," Nona had said after the nurse had led Vincent away, "there are probably a lot of crazy women pepper spraying innocent people." She gave Belana a withering glance.

"Nona, don't make things worse for yourself," Nick warned.

The same nurse finally returned with Vincent who was no longer holding the towel over his burning eyes. He was wearing a disposable pair of dark glasses.

"He should be fine now," the nurse said, "but he'll need to fill this prescription for eye ointment. He needs to use it for ten days. He'll have some redness, but there should be no scarring."

Relieved, Belana stood up and went to the nurse, holding her hand out for the prescription. "I'll make sure it gets filled."

Earlier, she had wanted to take care of Vincent's medical bill but Nick had insisted on paying, saying it would come out of Nona's allowance.

Nona went to Vincent and put her arm around his waist. "How're you feeling?"

"My eyes aren't burning anymore," Vincent said. "I don't know how I'm going to explain this to my mom and dad."

"Don't worry about that," said Nick. "We're all going over to your house and we'll take turns telling them what happened."

Vincent winced. "Mr. Reed, I know this looks bad but I really care about Nona. And for what it's worth, nothing happened."

"That's good," Nick told him, taking him by the arm. "Let's go tell your parents that."

Belana and Nick were exhausted by the time they and Nona got back to his place later that night. Vincent's parents had been livid that their son had been caught in a compromising position and they promised to punish him appropriately. He would be spending a lot of time visiting the elderly at area nursing homes. His mother was a nurse at one of them and knew the residents could do with a few youthful visitors who would willingly read to them or simply talk to them for a couple of hours per week.

Nick had phoned his mother and told her what happened. He told her Nona would be staying with him for the weekend. He would come up with a punishment for her sometime during the weekend.

At his apartment, Belana collected her belongings

that she'd left behind in their haste to get Vincent to a hospital, and left Nick and Nona alone.

She took a cab home and fell into her bed, ignoring her growling belly until the wee hours of the morning when it woke her and she opened a can of soup, warmed it and devoured the entire can.

At Nick's place Nona was ordered to bed. Her father would deal with her in the morning.

The next morning Nick still had not thought of a suitable punishment. They ate breakfast in silence and then he told her to go to her room and do the homework she'd brought home for the weekend. Nona told him she'd already done her homework.

"That's what's wrong," her father had said. "You have too much time on your hands. If you worked harder in school you wouldn't have time to be plotting how to lose your virginity. Maybe I ought to send you to an all-girl school."

Nona, who resented being punished when nothing had happened between her and Vincent mouthed off with, "Go ahead. I hear girls who go to all-girl schools manage to lose their virginity even faster than girls who go to coed schools."

Nick glared at her. "You honestly don't understand why I'm upset with you?"

She sat like a bump on a log.

"You know you were born to your mother and me when we were both only eighteen," Nick said.

His daughter nodded.

"Well, we were sixteen when we became sexually

active. We thought we knew everything and were prepared for the consequences, but we weren't, Nona. Your mother got pregnant and we panicked. She considered having a secret abortion…"

Nona's eyes stretched in horror.

"Yeah, that's right, you might not have even been born if she had," Nick continued. "But we were smart enough to go to our parents for advice and after all the yelling they promised that they would stand by us. We had you, and we got married shortly after you were born. Your mother's parents moved back down South so most of the responsibility of seeing us through it fell on your grandmother. My dad, whom you never knew because he died shortly after you were born, said the best thing to do was have us live with them. We moved in and we were still living in your grandmother's house when your mother, who had earned her teaching certification, went to visit her parents because her father was sick, and left you with me and your grandmother. She was killed in an accident on the way back."

Nona was crying.

"What I'm trying to say to you, Nona, is your mother and I worked hard so that you wouldn't have to struggle the way we did. We both wanted better for you and it would have broken her heart to see you going down the same road we did with your irresponsible behavior. Having sex at your age might seem like a good idea to you, but believe me, there are consequences."

Nona ran to her father and threw her arms around

his neck. "I'm sorry, Daddy! I'll be more responsible, I promise."

Nick held her tightly. "You're precious to me. You're all I have left of your mother. You're the product of our dreams for the future, don't you see that?"

Nona looked up into her father's eyes which were moist with tears. "I've got to apologize to Belana, too. I yelled at her. I said some awful things to her. I told her I hated her."

Nick smiled. "I'm sure she knows you didn't mean that. You love her. I can see it in your eyes whenever you look at her."

"I do love her," Nona said. "I wish I could take back what I said."

Chapter 12

On debut night, Belana tried to keep her focus entirely on her upcoming performance, but it was hard to do. She was emotionally fragile. Because of her tight rehearsal schedule she and Nick had not been able to spend more than a few minutes at a time together since the day she'd walked in on Nona and Vincent. Phone calls just weren't cutting it. Her relationship with Nona had improved, though. Nona came by her apartment one afternoon and apologized to her, saying she realized, now, that she had done a foolish thing and she and Vincent had agreed that it was too soon to be thinking of having sex. Belana had been relieved beyond words. However, her happiness was short-lived because that very night her father phoned and said Drusilla had taken ill and was in the hospital in New Haven. Her father and stepmother assured her it was nothing serious, just a stomach virus, but at Drusilla's age a stomach virus could lay her low. Therefore, her father and stepmother wouldn't be at the debut.

Elle and Patrice, with their families, would be in the audience, though; and Erik, who would be escorting Ana. They were still only friends but Belana saw it as a good sign that they were attending social events together more and more.

Nick promised that he, Nona and Yvonne would be there to cheer her on.

She was in her dressing room now, listening to the orchestra warming up. She was in full costume. Titania, queen of the fairies and wife of Oberon, king of the fairies, was a vision in white sprinkled with fairy dust. There was even glitter in her hair which was left unbound and flowing down her back as befitted the queen of the fairies.

She frowned at her reflection. The makeup, applied thickly as usual, was ethereal. She looked like an otherworldly spirit. The makeup artist had achieved this by making her brown skin glow, but making her features stand out in stark relief by painting her mouth white and sculpting her cheekbones to make them look as high as humanly possible. Her long, thick false eyelashes also glittered.

There was a knock at the door. She automatically glanced at the clock on the wall. It was too early for her five-minute warning. She had a full fifteen minutes before that.

She walked to the door and called through it, "Yes?"

"Miss Whitaker?" asked a feminine voice with a lilting tone.

"Yes?"

"It's your mother, Belana. Please, open the door."

Belana's stomach muscles constricted painfully. The blood drained from her face and her skin suddenly felt chilled. She touched the doorknob but stayed her hand, wondering if she truly wanted to open the door.

She was already at an emotional deficit worrying about Drusilla. Would she be able to perform after seeing the woman who had abandoned her twenty-six years ago? Yet, curiosity was eating away at her rationality. What could her mother want? Had she aged well? Was she alone or had she brought her husband, Henri, with her? Did she and Erik have half brothers and sisters whom they'd never heard of?

She wound up opening the door and standing aside for her mother to enter.

Mari Tautou entered on a cloud of Chanel no. 5. She was wearing a red designer suit with tan accessories. The sable coat she had on was a rich brown that matched the color of her eyes. She was as Belana remembered: petite perfection. She had not lost her figure and her face was unlined, although both could have been surgically enhanced, Belana thought pettily.

She closed and locked the door, then turned and

faced the woman who had negatively affected her life in spite of her attempts to prevent that from happening.

Mari Tautou smiled at her. "You make a beautiful Titania."

Belana recalled that Mari had danced the role for the first time more than twenty years ago and had reprised it at least two more times over the years. "I haven't seen or heard from you in over eighteen years. What are you doing here?"

"I came to see my daughter dance Titania," she said, her smile never wavering. "Is that so strange?"

"I'm sure you know that a dancer expresses her emotions on the stage. What possessed you to come here and upset me just before the debut?"

"It wasn't my intention to upset you," Mari denied. She removed her sable and held it with her arms folded in front of her, her chic little shoulder bag on her right shoulder. "I only wanted to see you and Erik. Finding you was easy since opening night is advertised in all the papers. But Erik wasn't as easy to track down. Will he be here tonight?"

Belana was having trouble wrapping her mind around this moment. It felt like a dream, surreal and yet too real. She continued to look at her mother, at the veneer of coolness etched on her face. How could anyone display such icy detachment?

"I assure you, Erik is not as eager to see you as you are to see him," she said after a while.

"Nonetheless," Mari said stubbornly, "since I'm here I'd like to see him, too."

"Do you think I actually care about what you want?" asked Belana, barely able to contain her irritation. "You don't just drop into somebody's life after eighteen years without a good explanation. I repeat: why are you here?"

Mari's gaze roamed around the room. "What a charming dressing room. It's much larger than the one I had when last I danced here." She walked over and sniffed the roses that Nick had sent her. "From an admirer?" she asked softly. "How sweet."

"Seriously," Belana said, walking over to the door and placing her hand on the doorknob, "I'm going to have security escort you off the premises if you don't tell me why you've come right now!"

"I'm not well," Mari said hurriedly. "I wanted to see you and Erik one more time before it was too late to see you." She looked at Belana beseechingly.

Belana peered at her with skepticism. The best ballerinas were good actresses. They had to convey emotions with their bodies that most people could not even express with words. She got closer to her mother. Close enough to see that the whites of her eyes were discolored. What she had thought was flawless skin was really achieved with the help of the skilled application of makeup. And her petite figure was a tad emaciated.

"What's wrong with you?" Belana asked, frowning with concern.

"It's nothing hereditary," said Mari quickly. "I have stage four lung cancer from smoking for over thirty years. You know how some of us smoke to curb our appetites. I began doing it and, alas, I got hooked. I hope you never picked up the habit, darling. It's a miracle I'm standing here, really."

Belana felt her body begin to tremble with pent-up emotion. This was horrible. Why had her mother waited until she was dying to come back? When it was too late to have any kind of relationship with her? It was the ultimate form of rejection as far as Belana was concerned, and the ultimate example of narcissism on her mother's part. Her mother got to have her wish fulfilled, that of seeing her children again. But her children would forever be denied the opportunity to know her.

Belana wanted to swear, but instead, calmly asked, "Where is your husband?"

Mari's eyes watered. "He died a year ago, from lung cancer, too. The ironic thing is he didn't even smoke." She looked toward the ceiling as tears left streaks down her face. "It's only fitting that I join him soon."

Belana cringed. Her mother blamed herself for her husband's death. How did anyone live with guilt of such magnitude? She wouldn't wish that kind of pain on her worst enemy. However, she couldn't bring herself to rush forward and offer her comfort. There was too big a chasm between them that would probably always be too wide to cross. She could give her what she'd come here for, though. "Excuse me," she said softly as she crossed the room and picked up her cell phone, which she'd left atop the vanity.

She punched in Erik's cell phone number.

"Belana, is something wrong?" Erik asked, sounding panicked. He knew she was getting ready to go on and she wouldn't be phoning him just to chat.

"Sweetie," Belana said, her voice cracking. "I have a visitor in my dressing room. It's our mother and she wants to see you. Will you come?"

Emotion thickened her brother's voice when he answered, "I'll be right there."

Belana hung up the phone and looked over at her mother. "He's on the way."

"Thank you," Mari said. "I know I don't deserve your kindness."

They waited in silence for the next couple of minutes. Then Belana said, "Now that I've done you a favor, would you reciprocate?"

"Anything," said Mari, and her eyes revealed her desperation to please.

"I can almost understand why you left. Daddy wanted a full-time wife and you had to be free to dance. I understand the compulsion to dance since I feel the same way and wouldn't want to be with a man who wanted me to give it up. But why didn't you even want to share custody of me and Erik? Why shut yourself off from us completely?"

"First of all, I have to clear up a misconception you have concerning your father," Mari began. "He was always supportive of my career. He would have gladly continued to support me. But I fell in love with Henri. I felt a passion for him that I didn't for your father. Because of that, I felt unworthy as a mother. I had left your father because I couldn't control my libido, or so I felt back then. And after I'd left I felt I'd made my bed, I had to lie in it. Therefore, I decided that a complete cut was for the best. You didn't need the influence of a faithless mother, and I didn't deserve your love."

"But you did influence me," Belana told her. "For years I wouldn't let myself get close to a man for fear I'd wind up hurting him like you hurt Daddy. I thought I didn't have the capacity for faithfulness."

This time Mari's tears were not silent. Her tiny body was racked with sobs. Belana went to her and cradled her in her arms. It was then it really hit home how fragile her mother was. Holding her was like holding a bird with brittle, hollow bones. That was when she started to cry.

She thanked God when Erik knocked on the door a short while later.

Instead of the heart-wrenching reunion with her mother depleting her and sending her into a downward spiral of depression, it served to buoy Belana's spirits and she danced beautifully on opening night. She felt as if she was dancing for both her mother and herself. The next day the ballet critic who had put the success of the show squarely on her shoulders was compelled to report that, *Belana Whitaker was the definitive Titania. I don't believe I've ever witnessed a more powerfully spiritual performance. I am privileged to have been in the audience last night. It was an experience I'll never forget.*

The show was sold out every night of its eight-week run. And Belana performed with as much vigor and passion as she had that first night.

Between rehearsals and performances, she and Erik spent time getting to know their mother. Initially, she was going to go back to Marseille after a few days' visit because she didn't want to be an imposition. Belana suspected it was because her strength was failing her and she didn't want to be a burden on them.

They were having dinner together at Belana's apartment one evening. Nick and Ana were there as well. Mari swallowed a mouthful of sautéed green beans and grimaced. She rose quickly. "Please excuse me," she said and fled to the bathroom. A moment later, Belana followed.

Erik followed Belana.

They heard their mother coughing so badly it sounded as if she might choke.

The bathroom door was closed but Belana tried the doorknob and discovered it was unlocked. She saw Erik behind her and motioned for him to stay there. When she got inside, her mother was hacking up blood into a wad of tissues.

"I'll call for an ambulance," Belana immediately cried, turning to leave.

Her mother reached out a hand and grasped her by the wrist. She coughed again into the tissues, and then seemed to get it under control. Raising her reddened eyes to Belana's she said in a hoarse voice, "They can't do anything for me, darling. I must go home."

"Who do you have at home to take care of you?" Belana asked.

"I have dear old friends," her mother answered.

"Dear old friends who're willing to be with you through it all?"

Her mother looked away and Belana knew she didn't really have anyone in Marseille who would be with her at the end. She couldn't bear to let her go back there to die alone.

"You'll stay with us," Belana said. "Erik and I will look after you."

Erik, who had been eavesdropping through the door Belana had left ajar, strode into the room. "Yes, we will. You don't have to endure this on your own."

After that incident Belana and Erik insisted, despite their mother's protests, that she be thoroughly examined by the noted cancer specialists at Memorial Sloan-Kettering Cancer Center. They prayed for a more optimistic prognosis than Mari's French doctors had given her, only to be disappointed.

Mari told them she was not saddened by this news. She had fulfilled her wish of seeing them again, and that's all that mattered to her. Two months after she showed up at Belana's dressing room door, she was admitted into Sloan-Kettering after she had trouble breathing in the night.

She died three hours later with Belana and Erik at her side.

At the memorial service held at the Abyssinian Baptist Church, Belana and Erik sat on the front row:

Nick at Belana's side and Ana at Erik's. Ana had proven to be as good a friend to him as he had been to her. Mari's name alone had drawn a crowd of hundreds. Even though she had been retired from dance for several years she was still thought well of in the dance community. Dance luminaries rose to speak of her accomplishments in glowing terms and tell how she had inspired them in some way. Belana barely heard what they said because her mind was in turmoil. She had known her mother so fleetingly. She did, however, hear the sobbing of someone behind her. It was Nona.

Later, after they'd gathered at a restaurant in Harlem for a buffet-style meal, Belana had pulled Nona aside to hug her and say, "Are you all right? I heard you crying at the service."

Nona forced a smile for Belana's benefit. She'd let her dreadlocks grow and now they were halfway down her back. "I feel so sad for you," she told Belana, "because I realize now why you never told me Mari Tautou was your mother. She broke your heart, and if I'd found out how badly she'd hurt you, I might have been discouraged in some way, given up my dream of one day being as good as she was." Tears ran fresh down her face. "My mother's gone and now yours is, too. We're both motherless, Belana!"

Nick happened to walk up at the tail end of his daughter's declaration and misunderstood the meaning behind it. He thought she was insensitively reminding Belana that her mother was dead. "Nona," he said quietly but fiercely. "Apologize at once."

"Nick," Belana said quickly. "She was just saying that she and I have that in common. She was trying to console me."

Nick immediately apologized to Nona. "I'm sorry, baby. It's been a stressful day."

Nona simply smiled. Her father had been watching her like a hawk ever since the Vincent incident. She really had to be on her p's and q's around him. He'd also been overprotective of Belana lately. He was wrong when he said it had been a stressful day. It had been a stressful *month*. She didn't know how Belana had danced six shows a week for eight solid weeks while her mother had been dying. But, she supposed, entertainers actually lived by the adage—the show must go on.

"Don't worry about it, Daddy," she said. "I think I'll go get something to drink."

After she'd gone, Belana said, "You've got to ease up on her. She's doing her best to make up for what she did."

Nick grimaced as he looked after his daughter. "I know, but I'm paranoid now and wonder if she's just telling me she's taken a vow of chastity. She's still going to the same school, and she's still friends with the same kids."

"Yes, but she's made up her mind. Your daughter is an indomitable young woman when she decides to do something. Have faith in her."

"I'm trying," said Nick.

"Try harder," Belana told him, and rose on her toes to plant a kiss on his cheek.

Drusilla, who had come to the memorial service with John and Isobel, walked up to Belana and Nick. "I always said I would dance on that woman's grave," she said of Mari as she leaned heavily on her cane. "Now, all I have is sympathy for her. I must really be getting old!"

Belana laughed in spite of herself. Leave it to Drusilla to inject humor into an otherwise sad day. Belana hugged her grandmother. "I love you. I hope you never change."

Drusilla smiled up at her. "I love you, too, baby." She sighed as she peered across the room at Erik and Ana, standing with John and Isobel. "Those two are still 'friends,'" she said with a touch of irritation. "I'm gonna have to light a fire under them."

She crooked her finger at Nick. He leaned down to hear what she had to tell him and she kissed him on the cheek. "You're a handsome devil."

Nick grinned. "Thank you, Mrs. Whitaker. You look lovely today yourself."

"You'd just as well call me Grandma," said Drusilla. "Practice for when you marry my granddaughter."

"Grandma, really," Belana protested. "No one's said anything about getting married."

"Well, somebody up in here *should* be talking about getting married," said Drusilla, getting her second wind. "What is it with you young people? I married your grandfather three weeks after I met him."

"Three weeks?" asked Nick, incredulously.

Belana had heard this story many times before. She wouldn't dream of interrupting her grandmother, though.

"Yes, three weeks," Drusilla confirmed. She shifted her weight. Belana thought she looked absolutely adorable in her black pantsuit and white blouse. *She* had on a sleeveless black dress and black pumps. The only jewelry she wore was a three-quarter-length pearl necklace.

"Veni, vidi, vici," intoned Drusilla.

Nick knew that meant, I came, I saw, I conquered, and wondered who had conquered whom. Knowing Drusilla, she had definitely been the conqueror.

"I knew I was going to marry that man the moment I laid eyes on him. He was a tall drink of water. Broad like an oak tree and, boy, did I have fun climbing him," Drusilla said loudly.

"Grandma, please keep your voice down," said Belana.

Drusilla did as she was told, but didn't quit talking. She winked at Nick. "There's nothing wrong with newlyweds enjoying each other. It's their God-given right."

She smiled at Belana. "I've embarrassed you enough for one day." She gestured for Belana to lean down. She kissed her granddaughter on the lips. "So sorry about your mother, darling. I'm going to have your parents take me home now."

"Thank you, Grandma," Belana said, hugging her warmly.

* * *

That evening Belana and Nick sat in one another's arms on her sofa with the music turned down low. Tomorrow was Saturday and for once in a long while neither of them had anywhere to be except with each other.

"You know, your grandmother was right about one thing today," said Nick softly in her ear.

Belana was so relaxed, the day's stresses having been vanquished by Nick's nearness, that she lazily asked, "Mmm?"

"That somebody should be talking about marriage," Nick reminded her.

Belana perked up.

"Although it might be too soon to be talking about marriage," said Nick, referring to the fact that she was still grieving her mother.

Belana was silent for a moment. After all the time her mother had wasted, she didn't believe she would want her to waste any. "No," she said, turning around to peer up into Nick's eyes. "It's not too soon. I don't think my mother would want me to postpone my life. She thought she had wasted too much time."

Nick smiled and said, "I've got to get up for this."

Belana let him go and tucked her legs under her as she watched him walk over to the hall tree, reach into his coat pocket and retrieve a small box covered in red velvet.

She felt a mixture of nervousness and excitement as he sat down beside her, opened the lid of the little red box and offered her the most beautiful diamond solitaire she'd ever seen. In a platinum setting, the stone was perfect and it was a tasteful five carats. He had known she didn't go for ostentatious displays of excess.

Their eyes met and held. "Belana, would you do me the honor of becoming my wife?"

Belana burst into tears. Maybe it was the stress of the day. Maybe it was because she knew how close she'd come to losing Nick forever. Maybe it was because she loved him so much she couldn't imagine life without him.

"Yes!" she cried. "I would love nothing more than to become your wife."

Nick grinned. Then he bent and kissed her until they were both dizzy from oxygen deprivation, and in that drunken, elated state, he put the ring on her finger.

After which they sealed the deal by making slow, sweet love right there on her couch.

Four months later, on a Saturday in June, they were married at her family's New Haven estate with two hundred people in attendance. Elle and new mother Patrice were her matrons of honor. T.K. sat in the front row with their son sleeping in his arms. Ana and Nona were two of her six bridesmaids. Ari was the sole flower girl, spreading rose petals along the aisle while guests sighed over how precious she was. She, being the daughter of two entertainers, ate it up and smiled prettily.

When the minister announced that Belana and

Nicolas were husband and wife, Drusilla yelled, "Hallelujah!"

At the reception, Belana and Nick cut the wedding cake which had been made by none other than Mrs. Lyla Daly. It was a traditional multitiered masterpiece with three different flavors of cake: lemon, vanilla, and red velvet covered in vanilla crème icing and decorated with lilacs.

Nick and Belana each had a morsel in their hands and they crossed arms and fed each other, not trying to smash the cake into each other's faces as they'd seen some newlyweds playfully do. No, they had no time for antics such as that. They could not take their eyes off each other. They wanted nothing more than to be alone but felt they must endure the rest of the day out of love and respect for their friends and family.

But after all the toasts had been said, and the bride had danced with her father, who was teary-eyed, they danced together and socialized for a while then at the first opportunity that presented itself, they snuck off and climbed into the waiting limousine that would take them to the New Haven luxury hotel where they would spend the night.

In the hotel suite, it took less than a minute to doff wedding attire that had seemed to take forever to get into. Then they were making love, skin against skin, mouths seeking succor and relentlessly finding it. Not saying a word, because their bodies spoke louder than words ever could.

She was his equal in every way, giving him all of her

because it would never occur to her to do less. Warm unyielding muscles felt like velvet-covered steel to her roaming hands. He was intoxicated by the silken texture, fragrance and sensuality of her skin.

He could not stop inhaling her scent, tasting her, reveling in the utter delight that touching her filled him with.

He held back as long as he could. He never wanted this ecstasy to end. But when she came and he heard that mewling sound she made at the back of her throat he also rushed over the precipice and they fell together. They hit the bed, as if they had actually fallen from a great height, and looked into one another's eyes.

"Felt like…" Belana said breathlessly.

"The first time," Nick finished for her.

They were lucky enough to stay in love the entire length of their marriage. In the second year they were blessed with a baby boy. They named him after his father who was a junior, so everyone called him Tre, pronounced *tray,* which was short for *tres,* Spanish for the number three. His sister, Nona, called him less complimentary names when he was just being a little brother, but he never let that bother him. He simply adored her.

Belana danced until she was thirty-three, working four years longer than she'd anticipated. Nick opened his own agency and while it might not have been the biggest agency in Manhattan, it represented some of the top athletes in the world.

When they had been married six years, Belana presented Nick with a daughter. They named her Mari Drusilla. Her great-grandmother, who had managed to dodge the Grim Reaper and was approaching eighty-eight took one look at her and said, "She looks just like me!"

Belana had smiled. Indeed, her daughter with her scrunched-up newborn face did look remarkably like a gnome. But she knew she would grow out of it and be as beautiful as the two women she'd been named for.

One night they left Mari Drusilla with her doting maternal grandparents and Nick took his wife to the ballet. They held hands and watched, rapt, as Nona danced her first solo with the New York City Repertory Dance Theatre. Later, Belana hugged her stepdaughter and said, "You danced beautifully."

And her stepdaughter beamed at her and said, "I learned from the best. My mom used to be a ballerina."

* * * * *

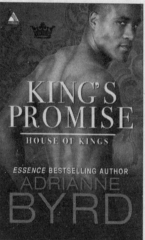